"Two days isn't exactly a lifetime, Jared."

Jared moved away from the doorframe and walked slowly toward Kate, his gaze mesmerizing. "It depends who you spend those two days with." He took her into his arms, kissing her with a drugging hunger.

"I haven't been able to get you out of my mind," he muttered raggedly against her throat before his mouth claimed hers again, deepening the caress with probing warmth.

"No!" Kate wrenched away from him, her hands shaking. "I'm going to marry Richard."

"I don't happen to agree with you," Jared challenged. "You see, I intend marrying you myself."

Kate searched his rugged features for signs of madness. She'd already had a sample of men like Jared. No man, not even this charming rogue, would use her as a meal ticket again.

Books by Carole Mortimer

These books may be available at your local bookseller.

For a free catalog listing all titles currently available,
send your name and address to:

Harlequin Reader Service
P.O. Box 52040, Phoenix, AZ 85072-2040
Canadian address: Stratford, Ontario N5A 6W2

CAROLE MORTIMER

sensual encounter

Harlequin Books

TORONTO • NEW YORK • LONDON
AMSTERDAM • PARIS • SYDNEY • HAMBURG
STOCKHOLM • ATHENS • TOKYO • MILAN

For
John and Matthew

Harlequin Presents first edition April 1984
ISBN 0-373-10684-X

Original hardcover edition published in 1983
by Mills & Boon Limited

CHAPTER ONE

'. . . and this new account could be really important to the agency,' Kate was telling Richard as she came through from the kitchen with the ice for their drinks, her long flaming red hair secured in a classical style at her nape. 'Whisky?' she queried in a preoccupied voice.

'And a little ice only,' the man seated on the luxurious sofa requested, his fine dinner suit obviously from Savile Row, the cufflinks at his wrist gold, his shoes handmade. Richard James was a rich man, and he looked it, from his styled dark hair to his Italian shoes.

And Kate liked rich men, rich and powerful men. She more than liked Richard, she intended marrying him. Fortunately, it looked as if he felt the same way.

'Thank you, darling.' He looked up at her with dark eyes, admiring everything about the beautiful woman who was to be his wife, preferring the elegance of her severe hairstyle to a softer styling, the bright red hair dulled to copper, her eyes a wide almond shape, golden in colour, slightly tilted at the corners, her cheekbones high, emphasised by a light blusher, her nose short and straight, the wide bow of her mouth outlined in a deep plum lip-gloss, the black dress she wore as sophisticated as the other clothes she bought from one of his exclusive shops in town. He must remember to open an account for her as soon as possible—beside the fact that he intended marrying her, no one who could do such justice to the dresses deserved to pay for them! Kate was everything he

7

could possibly want in a wife. 'I have a table booked for eight—Are you expecting anyone?' he frowned as the doorbell pealed in Kate's apartment.

'No.' She put her glass down, her hand long and elegant, the nails painted the same plum colour as her lipgloss. 'Perhaps it's Gill from downstairs, she's always running out of things for some reason,' the last was added with irritation, her own methodical way of life not allowing for such occurrences. Head of an advertising agency, she had to live her life that way, both privately and professionally, clients and employees depending on her.

'Don't let her keep you long,' Richard's hand trailed intimately down her arm. 'We have to leave for the restaurant in a few minutes.'

Kate's expression was thoughtful as she went to the door. If it were Gill she hoped she was returning the set of vegetable dishes she had borrowed for a special dinner last month; she could be needing them herself soon!

She had no premonition as she opened the door, no warning of the shock she was to receive when she saw the identity of her visitor. Her mouth fell open in surprise, her face paling, the golden eyes suddenly huge in her drawn face.

At that moment she wished she could deny all knowledge of the man standing outside the door, but the lean body in the casual denims and short leather jacket, the ruggedly attractive face dominated by laughing blue eyes, the overlong dark hair with its auburn highlights were all too familiar. Jared Rourke!

'Hello, Kate,' he greeted softly, in a well-educated voice, although it did not indicate public school like Richard's did.

She wished she could have answered him, but for the moment she seemed to have lost her voice— something that had never happened to her before.

What was he *doing* here? More to the point, what was she going to do with him when Richard was waiting for her in the lounge?

Jared felt no such inhibitions about his own actions, and stepped forward, taller than her by at least six inches at six foot two, his arms like steel vices as he took her in his arms, his mouth claiming hers with arrogant possession.

Kate felt herself respond to him as she had from their first meeting, having no strength to fight him as his mouth moved over hers with drugging insistence, laying intimate claim to her lips, while his hands moved over her body with sure deliberation.

'Mm,' he pulled back slightly, resting his forehead on hers as he looked down at her, a growth of copper-coloured beard on his chin evidence of his need of a shave. 'I needed that,' he spoke softly, his voice husky. 'I was sure I must have imagined how good it was with you, but now I know I didn't!'

'Jared——'

'Mmm,' he kissed her again, 'you're beautiful, Kate. I'd forgotten how beautiful.' Large hands touched the smoothness of her hair. 'Or I just thought I'd imagined that too. What did we have, Kate? Two days, two long glorious days when we——'

'Please, Jared,' she pushed firmly against the hard wall of his chest, looking up at him with steady gold eyes. 'What we had really isn't important.'

The blue eyes narrowed. 'Not important? How can you say that? We——'

'Darling, what is it?' Richard appeared behind her, looking pointedly at his gold wrist-watch. 'We have to leave soon,' he reminded her.

Kate swallowed hard, looking anxiously at the two men. Richard was obviously unaware of the tension between them, his brows raised at Jared in polite query. But Jared was the one causing most of the tension—*all* of it!—and his flinty blue eyes were narrowed back at Richard.

'This gentleman was looking for Gill,' Kate hurried into speech, hearing the words in some disbelief, sure she couldn't really have spoken them. But what was she supposed to say, what *could* she say? This is a perfect stranger I spent two days with three months ago? No, she couldn't say that, and she hoped Jared would have enough decency not to say it either.

He remained silent, although his mocking blue eyes passed from her to Richard, and then back again.

'Well, don't be long, darling.' Richard spoke impatiently. 'It shouldn't take all night to explain that Gill lives in the flat below.' He turned and returned to the lounge to finish his drink, obviously considering the matter settled.

But it was far from being that! Jared crossed his arms across his chest, leaning casually against the door-frame. 'Who was *that*?' he drawled.

Kate flushed at his derisive tone. 'Richard is a friend——'

'I gathered that—*darling!*'

Her eyes flashed like molten gold. 'Then you must also have gathered that your presence here is a complete surprise to me.' She gripped her hands tightly together in front of her, the rigidity of her shoulders thrusting her breasts forward beneath the black dress, the nipples hardened in her emotional tension.

'It is?' He raised dark brows, the dark lashes about deep blue eyes ridiculously long for a man. 'You surely didn't think I was going to disappear out of your life?'

'Why not?' she snapped tautly. 'You have for the last three months.'

'I told you I was going to North America; it was something I couldn't get out of. But I asked you to come with me,' he reminded her.

'Yes, well——' she avoided his searching gaze, 'I had no intention of hitch-hiking around Canada for three months with a man I'd only just met!'

'Hitch-hiking?' he repeated with a frown. 'Who said anything about hitch-hiking?'

Her gaze moved scathingly over his casual attire, the faded denims even patched in a couple of places. He was decidedly out of place in the tasteful elegance of her home, the exact opposite of Richard's sophistication, despite the fact that the two men were of a similar age, both in their mid-thirties.

'Oh, I see,' Jared derided tauntingly as he correctly read her scorn. 'You don't think I'm capable of affording any other form of transport. Are you a snob, Katharine Mary Collier?' His eyes were narrowed again.

'No, of course not!' She flushed in spite of herself. 'You told me yourself that you live on your wits, and I just——'

'Don't believe in roughing it with someone like me when you can ride around with friend Richard in the Porsche. That is his car outside, isn't it?' he mocked.

'Yes. But——'

'Nice car.'

'He thinks so,' she said stiffly.

'And you, do you think so too?' His voice was taut.

'Of course,' she bit out. 'Look, Mr Rourke——'

'Mr?' he derided mockingly. 'Really, Kate, you're being ridiculous now. I doubt your *friend* can hear us out here, it's quite safe to call me Jared when we're alone.'

'All right, Jared,' bright spots of angry colour darkened her cheeks, her eyes gleaming, 'Richard *is* my friend, and why you've had to come here and try and cause trouble I have no idea.'

His eyes widened. 'What trouble have I tried to

cause? I wasn't to know you would have your boy-friend here.'

'You could have called first!'

'It took me long enough to find out your real name and address, let alone your telephone number!'

'*How* did you find out my name and address?' she frowned.

'It wasn't easy,' he shrugged. 'But I remembered you said you were in advertising. I have a few connections in the business world,' he ignored her scathing snort, 'people who owe me a few favours. Luckily there aren't too many redhaired beauties like you in advertising. It was a simple matter to visit all the ones who fitted the description. You were third on the list.'

'The fact that I did give you a false name should have told you something,' she snapped.

'Oh, it did,' he nodded unconcernedly. 'It told me you didn't mind spending a couple of days with me, but you didn't want any of your high-class friends to find out about it.'

Kate glanced towards the lounge with a hunted look in her eyes. 'Will you please keep your voice down?' she hissed vehemently. 'I don't want Richard to hear.'

'No, we mustn't have that, must we?' he taunted. 'Tell me, Kate——'

'Darling, are we—Are you still here?' Richard frowned his irritation as he saw the other man at the door. 'Hasn't Kate explained to you that Gill lives downstairs?' His arm went possessively about her slender waist.

'Kate's explanation was very exact,' Jared told the other man tautly.

'Then if you'll excuse us,' Richard said haughtily, 'we happen to be going out.'

Kate bit her lip anxiously at the derogatory tone of Richard's voice. One thing she had learnt about Jared

Rourke, if he had something to say then he said it. Richard's disdainful attitude was guaranteed to spark the Irish temper lurking in the icy blue eyes. She waited for the explosion that would ruin all her carefully laid plans, plans that would make her Richard's wife. But not if Jared told him about their meeting three months ago, not if he told him about the two days—and nights—they had spent together.

'Then I won't keep you any longer.' Jared pushed away from the doorframe in one lithe movement. I mustn't keep Gill waiting,' he added wickedly.

Richard looked uncomfortable at the suggestive tone in the other man's voice. 'Er—no. Well, glad to have been able to help you, Mr——?'

'Rourke,' Jared supplied, his expression mocking as he looked at Kate. 'Thank you, Miss Collier. I'll tell Gill how helpful you've been.'

Kate was left with the impression that it was a possibility that Jared would tell Gill exactly that—and he didn't even know Gill! Not yet, anyway. She knew from experience that that wasn't necessarily a drawback as far as Jared was concerned; once he made his mind up to do something he did it, regardless. It could be Gill's lucky night—if she liked attractive Irishmen, that is. Strangely that thought didn't please Kate at all.

He gave a brief wave of his hand as he stepped into the lift, his blue eyes burning with mocking mischief as he pressed the button to close the doors. Kate watched the lift floor numbers above the doors, her mouth tightening as it stopped on the floor below. Damn him, he *was* going to see Gill! He had gone to all the trouble of seeking her out, and now he had gone to the flat of a woman he didn't even know.

She closed the door with forceful anger, wondering why Jared should go through the lengthy process of finding her only to meekly leave again. It didn't seem like the man she knew. But going to see Gill he was! She knew better than most what a sensual man Jared Rourke was, how much he enjoyed women.

'Odd-looking man,' Richard said thoughtfully.

Kate gave him a sharp look. 'Odd?' she questioned his choice of word.

'Well, he must be my age,' Richard derided with a twist of his lips, 'and yet he looked like some damned hippie.'

Jared's casual clothing hardly made him a hippie, in fact the tight denims suited him, as did the rakish hairstyle, the leather jacket emphasising the width of his shoulders. She had forgotten his shoulders were that broad, his waist that narrow, his hips so powerful, his legs long and lean. Damn him, why did he have to be so attractive!

'Hippies went out years ago,' she snapped her agitation.

'Exactly,' Richard drawled derisively.

For the first time in weeks Kate felt irritation with him. 'Nothing about Mr Rourke looked outdated to me,' she said tautly.

He seemed not to notice her lack of good humour, glancing at his wrist-watch once again. 'We really will have to go now, Kate.' He held out the silver jacket that complemented the simplicity of style of her black dress and matched the colour of her sandals and evening bag. Richard knew he could never fault Kate's way of dressing, everything she wore was stylish and complimentary to her slender beauty—even creations that didn't belong to his stores!

If Richard could have read her thoughts at that moment he would have been a little shocked by her thoughts. She was remembering a time not so long ago when her clothes had been as casual as Jared Rourke's, of walking on a golden beach in her tight denims, her anorak stained with sea-spray. It was a memory she had tried to put out of her mind; seeing Jared again had reminded her of a lot of things she would rather forget.

'Yes, let's go.' She put her arm through the crook of his. 'I've been looking forward to our evening together.'

Richard looked pleased by her eagerness, and he visibly preened as they went down in the lift, liking the way she clung to his arm. Although he didn't look quite so happy when he saw the way a red Lamborghini had trapped him into his parking space. 'Damn,' he frowned at the rakish angle of the red car, before getting in behind the wheel of the Porsche to manoeuvre it slowly out on to the road with Kate's guidance from outside.

Kate glanced up to Gill's flat, wondering if Jared was going to be out of luck a second time tonight; the Lamborghini probably belonged to Gill's new boy-friend, the one she was trying so hard to impress.

They weren't having a very good start to what was supposed to be a special evening, Kate thought ruefully as they finally got started on the drive to the restaurant. Tonight she and Richard were having a celebration dinner; it was just like Jared Rourke to turn up and disturb her. Three months he had had to put in an appearance, and he had to turn up tonight of all nights!

But he had a way of doing that—hadn't his unexpected appearance been the reason she had met him in the first place?

The south-western coast of England in mid-March was not where she had intended to be three months ago, in fact she had intended being somewhere else completely at the time. But circumstances had dictated that she had to get away, and the hotel where she had spent many holidays with her parents as a child had appeared like a refuge when the yearly brochure had arrived in the post, a ritual that had continued despite the fact that she hadn't been there in five years.

It was a large impersonal hotel in one of the large coastal towns of Devon, providing many sporting or intellectual entertainments if you wanted them, but leaving you free to just be on your own if you preferred that. Kate did. She wanted to be alone. But on her first evening there she had met Jared Rourke, had met him at a time when all her defences were down. That was the excuse she had given herself over the months to explain her behaviour with him.

She had walked down to the secluded cove a short distance from the hotel, the sand silver-gold in the moonlight, the sea battling with the cliffs that prevented it sweeping overland to cause destruction in its wake. The chilling water had been cold about her ankles, the rest of her huddled down in warm clothing as the elements echoed her mood, stormy. When she walked into the solid object blocking her pathway she couldn't hold back her gasp of surprise.

'Did I hurt you?' queried a concerned voice from the darkness.

'You startled me!' She moved away from the bulky figure of the man, stepping back in the dry sand. She had thought herself alone.

'I didn't think you could startle pixies,' the man mused in that slightly lilting voice.

Kate gave an impatient sigh; she was not in the mood for a flirtation. 'If you'll excuse me,' she turned away, 'I have to get back to the hotel.'

'Why?'

She turned back to find him standing very close to her, the wind whipping her long red hair about her face as she tried to distinguish his features in the darkness. It was an impossible task. 'I just do,' she said irritably, and began to walk across the sand to the narrow pathway that led up to the hotel grounds.

A hand came out to grasp her arm, the man was still at her side. 'I'll walk with you.'

The voice sounded young, interested, and for the first time she realised the inadvisability of coming down here alone in the dark. 'Would you please leave me alone?' She pulled away from him.

'No.'

Kate swallowed hard at that single-worded answer. He spoke so firmly, so inevitably, that she felt her tension rising. 'I shall scream——'

'Who would hear you?' There was laughter in his voice now.

She moistened her lips, tasting the salt there, the sea-water being whipped up into the air by the fierce wind causing the whitecaps far out to sea being illuminated by the moon. If only she could see her accoster—all she knew was that he looked big and sounded young, his hair obviously long and dark as it was blown about. 'I didn't come alone,' she told him with confidence. 'I have a friend——'

'I know—me.' Once again he clasped her arm. 'I know you're down here alone, at the hotel alone too. Don't you realise how dangerous it could be out here?'

'I'm beginning to!'

'You're in no danger from me, I can assure you,' he mused.

'I'm not?' She unwittingly showed her uncertainty.

'Not at this precise moment, no,' he mocked. 'Later I can't answer for,' he added softly. 'I'm staying at the hotel too,' he spoke briskly. 'I saw you leave over an hour ago, when you didn't come back I thought I ought to come and check that you were okay.'

'Who asked you to be my watchdog?' Kate snapped.

'No one,' he replied without rancour. 'I just didn't like the picture I'd conjured up of you a helpless crumpled heap at the bottom of the cliff.'

'Well, you can see I'm fine, so I——'

'I'll just see you back to the hotel, if you don't mind.'

'I do!'

'Well, I'm going back myself anyway, so I might as well walk with you.'

'I——' Kate began.

'Are you here on holiday?' he asked conversationally. 'Only you don't seem to be with anyone and——'

'Are you spying on me?' she demanded furiously, turning to glare at him in the darkness, her eyes almost luminous, deep gold in her anger.

'Yes.'

'I—You——' She was speechless at his candidness.

'I saw you arrive this morning and I've been watching you ever since. I can't seem to do anything else,' he added derisively.

Now she knew who he was, knew the face and body behind the voice. She had been aware of a man with laughing blue eyes watching her as she brought in her cases this morning, and again as she ate dinner this evening. The man had been seated across the room from her, also alone. He was good-looking if you liked rakish charm and a complete disregard for fashion and elegance. He was also the last person she wanted to talk to, his interest in her being obvious as his gaze never left her during dinner. In fact, it had been this that had hastened her departure from the dining-room this evening, her meal only half over.

'How interesting,' she said in a bored voice, relieved as she saw the lights of the hotel.

'You don't think so?' he mocked.

'No.' She spoke with the same bluntness he did.

'It was a man,' he said with a sigh.

Kate came to a halt, looking up at him in the darkness. 'What was?' she queried warily.

'The reason you're spending time in a half empty hotel in mid-March.'

'Oh, but it isn't going to be half empty for long,' she derided. 'Apparently there's some sort of conference starting at the end of the week; I have to vacate my room then.'

'Good business management,' he murmured appreciatively. 'I often wondered how these big hotels at seaside resorts survived through the winter.'

'Well, now you know,' she taunted as he held the door open for her, the lighted reception area showing she had been right about his identity; he was the man with the laughing blue eyes and the teasing smile that made the waitress blush as she served him his meal.

'I certainly do.' Again he seemed unaffected by her rudeness. 'Would you like to join me in the bar for a drink?'

'No, thank you.' She pushed her long red hair away from her face, slightly wet from the damp air outside.

His mouth twisted. 'It *was* a man, wasn't it, the reason you're hiding yourself here?'

'I'm not hiding anywhere!' she snapped.

'No?' he taunted.

'No!' Her eyes glowed her anger, there was a healthy colour to her cheeks from her walk on the beach.

'Then have a drink with me.' He thrust his hands into the back pockets of his denims, looking at her challengingly.

She was being goaded into accepting, she knew that, and yet something made her want to accept that challange, to show herself that she might have been hurt by one man but she was still capable of attracting another one. 'I'll have a glass of brandy, thank you,' she accepted haughtily.

If he was surprised by her change of mind then he didn't show it, seeing her seated at one of the plush booths before going up to the bar to get their drinks. Kate compared his attire to the formality of some of the other men in the room, and found him wanting, although he seemed unconcerned, carrying himself with a confidence that said to hell with convention.

'Here we go.' He put their two brandy glasses down on the table, sitting close to her in the booth. 'Now tell me about yourself.' He sat forward, his elbow on the table bringing him very close to her.

She avoided his gaze. 'There's nothing to tell.'

'You come from London.'

'So do you,' she guessed in return. 'So what are you doing here?'

'It's off-season——'

'And the rates are lower,' she finished derisively.

'There is that,' he grinned. 'Although I was going to say there were fewer people.'

'Of course you were,' she mocked.

'Don't you get tired carrying that around with you?' He looked at her consideringly.

This time she was ready for him. 'The scowl or the chip on my shoulder?' she asked with sarcasm.

He began to smile, then he chuckled, and finally he laughed. 'I like a woman with a quick mind.'

'Only a quick mind?' she heard herself asking, putting the glass of brandy down with a shaking hand as she realised the brandy on an empty stomach was starting to make her head swim. She hadn't wanted her food earlier, and the glow spreading through her body reminded her of that fact. 'I think perhaps I should go——'

He stayed her with his hand on her arm. 'Don't,' he said huskily. 'Stay,' he encouraged softly. 'Tell me your name.'

Why shouldn't she stay and talk to him? Brian certainly wouldn't be pining away for her. Brian. She had tried not to think of him today, and she felt sure this handsome man with the devil in his eyes could help her to continue not to think of him.

She picked up her glass and drank some more of the brandy, feeling her recklessness grow with each mouthful. 'My name is Kate,' she told him throatily.

'Just Kate?' He raised dark brows.

'Just Kate,' she nodded, deciding there was no reason for him to know anything else about her.

He smiled. 'Then I'm just Jared.'

'That suits me. Would you like another drink?' she offered after swallowing down the last of her brandy.

'An independent woman, hmm?'

'Very much so,' she agreed tautly.

He sat back in a relaxed pose. 'Then I'd love another drink.'

Kate never knew afterwards how much she had had to drink during the evening, or quite what they talked about, but suddenly it was after eleven and Jared was suggesting walking her back to her room. Only he didn't want to leave her at the door, and it had nothing to do with the brandy that she invited him in.

The double bed that dominated the room added intimacy to the moment, and Jared seemed to become aware of it at the same time she did, their gazes locking and holding, the move into each other's arms made simultaneously, their lips meeting in a quest for mutual need, for forgetfulness on Kate's part.

She had known the moment he identified himself on the beach that the evening was going to end this way, knowing a need to feel wanted, to feel a woman, to know that it had nothing to do with her own attraction that had so suddenly changed Brian towards her.

.What she hadn't been prepared for had been her reaction to a man she only knew as Jared! Brian was the man she loved, but even he had only made her feel contented in her response to him, her real pleasure being in knowing she had pleased him. This man wasn't prepared to settle for contentment, his lips and hands ravaging her body in a fiery quest, taking her higher than she had ever wanted to go before.

Jared didn't rush a thing; each inch of her body was given his own brand of lovemaking, encouraging Kate to know each tautly muscled line of his body in return, their bodies finally melting together in such accord that she gasped at the pleasure of it, measuring the movements of her body to the smooth thrusts of Jared's, clutching on to the dampness of his shoulders as she arched into him in gasping ecstasy.

Jared had been insatiable that night, and for two more days and another night too, and while in his arms Kate hadn't been able to think of anything but him. She had let him take control of her life for the time she was with him, hadn't wanted to think of the reason she had come to the hotel in the first place, or of the lonely weeks ahead of her when she returned to London. She hadn't wanted to think of Brian either, or of the way he had hurt her. And she hadn't; she had given herself completely to Jared for the time they were together.

But the time for her to leave had arrived all too quickly, and with it the fact that she was Katharine Collier, the twenty-four-year-old owner of an up-and-coming advertising agency, and certainly beyond a clandestine affair with a man who didn't look as if he had ever worn a dinner suit in his life.

They had talked little during their time together, preferring to communicate with their bodies, and when Jared had asked to see her once he had returned to London she hadn't known what to say. Jared had proved himself to be an intelligent man, with a lively sense of humour, and a sensitivity that often made her cry out for mercy—a mercy she neither desired or was ever granted. But he was far removed from her life in London, and the thought of seeing him again there wasn't something she wanted.

That last day together they had lunched together in the dining-room, the staff politely ignoring the fact that they hadn't been seen for two days and serving them quietly and efficiently. But Jared's desire to see her when they returned to London made her wish that the meal was over and she were driving back to London.

'I'll be very busy for the next few weeks,' she said awkwardly. 'This holiday was unexpected, and I won't have time for socialising when I get back.'

'Who said anything about socialising?' He gave her a wicked grin, the eyes that could caress at a glance glowing with humour as he held her hand across the table. 'I like having you all to myself.'

She pulled her hand out from under his. 'I won't have time for that either,' she made her tone casual. 'I'm a working girl, remember?'

'And I'm sure you're excellent at it, darling.' He had taken to using the endearment during their time together, and he did it so naturally, casually, that Kate couldn't possibly object. 'But I won't be in London for several months yet myself; I have work of my own to do first.'

Her eyes widened. 'You do?'

'Yes,' he laughed at her surprised expression. 'I don't spend all my time making love to beautiful ladies. I have to earn a living too.'

'How?' She was interested in spite of herself.

'By my wits, mainly.'

His answer *didn't* surprise her. Jared had spent the last two days with her without thought or excuse to anyone, and when they had bothered to dress it had been informally, always denims and a casual shirt for Jared, not even a trace of the formal about the man who had been her lover for the last two days. He was a drifter, a man who admitted to living on his wits; he didn't fit in with her London lifestyle at all.

'What do you intend doing that will keep you away from London?' She pretended interest in a way of life that was totally alien to her.

He shrugged. 'I'll be in North America for the next few months. I have—Why don't you come with me?' he suggested with sudden excitement. 'Why didn't I think of it before? We don't have to part now, we could—Yes?' he looked up as a waiter appeared quietly beside their table.

'For you, Mr Rourke.' The man held out a tray with a message lying on its surface. He stood silently beside them waiting for a reply as Jared read the message.

Jared scanned the words with impatience. 'Damn,' he muttered before turning to face Kate. 'I have to go and make a call—do you mind?'

'Not at all,' she smiled, very conscious of the still-hovering waiter.

'We'll talk about North America when I get back.' He stood up to place a light kiss on her lips. 'I don't intend letting you escape me, Katharine Mary Collins.'

She had smiled tautly until he was out of the room, then she had sprung into action, hurriedly leaving the dining-room to pay her bill and collect her luggage, leaving the hotel before Jared realised she had gone, little dreaming that he would trace Kate Collins back to Kate Collier, never dreaming that he would want to.

What she had done, spending two days with a complete stranger, was out of character for her, an impetuous need for emotional reassurance after Brian had let her down so callously, but she doubted it was out of character for Jared. There was an experience about him that couldn't be denied, a knowledge of women that had been infinitely satisfying but which spoke of relationships with many different women. At the thirty-four she knew him to be that wasn't surprising, but she had known only one man before him, the man who had been the reason for her need to get away from London and all the well-meaning friends who would pity her to her face and laugh at her behind her back. What Brian had done, using her until someone more useful came along, was one of the oldest tricks in the book; and she had been so much in love she hadn't even realised what he was doing.

But Jared Rourke wasn't really her type, he had just been available when she needed him, and she didn't want to see him again. Once he was 'living on his wits' in North America he would realise she wasn't his type either.

She had really thought Jared would realise that, that she would never see him again. She certainly hadn't expected him to turn up at her flat, and not tonight of all nights. He had almost ruined everything. He still could; she doubted she had seen the last of Jared Rourke—even if he had gone to see Gill!

She couldn't believe he actually had the audacity to go through with that—could she? She could believe anything of him! She could even believe he would persuade Gill into believing she knew him . . .!

'Darling?'

She turned to find Richard frowning at her. They had stopped at the restaurant and the doorman was waiting for them to get out of the car. 'Sorry,' Kate forced a bright smile, dragging herself back to the present, to the man at her side, the man she had decided to marry. 'I'm hungry, aren't you?' she prompted lightly, stepping out of the car.

She swept into the restaurant at Richard's side, aware that they attracted considerable attention as they moved through the room to their table. Richard was a well-known personality in the City. And she knew that some of the attention was directed at her, that her elegant beauty attracted admiration. It wasn't ego that told her this, it was Richard himself. He had a reputation for escorting only beautiful women, and they had been seeing each other for almost two months now.

'Champagne,' he ordered imperiously of the wine waiter as he came to take their order, selecting a good year automatically, his knowledge of wines being as polished as the rest of him. 'To us,' he toasted her with warm brown eyes once their champagne had been poured. 'You realise you've made me the happiest man in London?'

'Only in London?' she taunted huskily.

'In the whole world,' he laughed softly, reaching into the pocket of his black dinner jacket to pull out a small black velvet ring-box. 'Can I place this ring on your finger, darling?' He opened the box to reveal a huge diamond set on a platinum band.

For only a brief moment Kate hesitated, then she held out her hand, putting both Brian and Jared out of her mind as Richard placed the ring on the third finger of her left hand.

CHAPTER TWO

RICHARD JAMES had become a customer of her agency six months ago, and had begun to pursue her immediately, the advertising they were doing for his numerous high-class clothing stores for women giving him a good excuse for seeing Kate often.

But six months ago Brian Linton had been very much a part of her life, and her rebuffs to Richard, although polite, had been exactly that.

But she had made a decision three months ago, and she had stuck to it. Brian had found himself a rich woman to marry, so she would marry well too. When she got back to London three months ago Richard had been in Europe on a promotional tour, but as soon as he returned last month she had shown him, without being too obvious, that she was no longer averse to his attentions. With a sophistication she had soon learnt was second nature to him he had begun a slow wooing, starting with flowers and small gifts, working up to the suggestion of a casual evening together to discuss his advertising. The subject of advertising hadn't been mentioned once during the whole evening, and when he asked to see her again she had willingly agreed. The wooing no longer went slowly after that. Yesterday he had asked her to marry him, and once again Kate hadn't hesitated.

She hadn't allowed for the fact that Jared might demand readmission to her life. Richard was well aware of the fact that she and Brian had been intimate—at twenty-four he didn't demand virginity from her!—but she doubted he would understand her affair with Jared. Was Jared the type to kiss and tell?

27

She didn't think so, although if he made any more unexpected appearances at her flat like tonight Richard might become suspicious of the fact that Jared was looking for Gill at all. If he came back—and Kate felt sure he would—she would just have to make sure he understood that their time together meant nothing to her, that she didn't want to see him again. Richard was the man in her life now, and he would remain the only man.

'Do you realise how happy you've made me?' He held the hand that bore his ring, taking it to his lips to kiss her palm. 'When can we be married?'

She blotted everything out of her mind but Richard and their wedding plans. 'When would you like to be married?'

'Tonight.' His dark gaze held hers.

She laughed softly. 'That's a little too soon for me. Would next month do?'

'If it has to,' he grimaced. He was not the most patient of men when it came to getting something he wanted.

'I think so, Richard.' She was suddenly serious. 'I told you about this new account I'm trying to acquire—I'd like to settle that before we're married.'

'Isn't Melfords a little high for you to aim, darling?' He quirked dark brows. 'After all, it's a multi-million-pound perfume industry.'

'And I'm just a small not-very-well-known agency.' She spoke the words he hadn't. If there was one thing about Richard that annoyed her—and it was the only thing!—it was the way he liked to underestimate her work, treating her career almost like a hobby she would soon tire of. He was of the old school, a wife was to adorn his house and table, to warm his bed and body, not to go out to work or have a career of her own. But the agency was hers, she had worked it up from nothing into a successful business, and she had no intention of giving it up, not now or when they were married. 'There was a rumour that Melfords were no longer satisfied with the work Hazeldene was doing for them. I made enquiries, and they didn't deny the rumour. At the moment they haven't said yes to the new ideas I sent them, but neither have they said no. The head of their advertising department told me that they're considering them.'

'Considering them, darling,' Richard drawled. 'You really mustn't get your hopes up too high.'

Kate had told herself the same thing, but the fact that her ideas were even being considered had given her hope. If she did get the contract—and she was well aware it was only an if—then the fee she would receive for her work would make her a very rich woman in her own right. It would be the final irony if Brian had left her for nothing, if she had as much money as the rich widow he had made his wife.

'I stand as much of a chance as anyone else,' she told Richard confidently. 'I have a good reputation, and some well-known and satisfied customers.'

'But none as big as Melfords,' he reasoned.

'Perhaps not,' she conceded, knowing that Richard's own company was the largest on her books, a fact he was probably aware of too. 'But maybe that's why I stand a chance. All the big agencies tend to have similar ideas; I pride myself on my originality. You're satisfied with your advertising, aren't you, darling?' she asked lightly.

'Of course,' he flushed. 'Although I have to admit I would have given you the contract even if I weren't; I was determined to have you from the first, Kate.'

'Thank you,' she smiled, although his words didn't please her. She knew he meant to flatter, and yet in doing so he took away from her achievement as a businesswoman. 'And now you have me, are you going to feed me?' she mocked him.

'Of course.' He straightened. 'We must celebrate our engagement properly, mustn't we?'

And celebrate they did, going on to a club after their meal, dancing until the early hours of the morning when Kate told Richard she really would have to get home. Tomorrow was a working day for her, and although she was the boss she wasn't just a figurehead, but took an interest in all of her clients, her personal service being part of the rapidly growing success of the agency. Clients didn't like to feel that anyone was inaccessible to them, she had learnt over the years.

It was after two when they arrived at her flat, and Richard declined coming in for coffee, arranging to see her the following day. His decision not to come in pleased Kate; until that moment she had been unsure of what he would expect of her now that she wore his ring. From their first date she had made it clear that she had no intention of going to bed with him, and although he had respected that up to now she hadn't been sure if it would still apply. He had clearly shown her that it did.

Her kiss goodnight was all the more passionate in her gratitude; she had decided, after the way Brian had taken advantage of her, and her impetuous time with Jared, that any other man that desired her now was going to have to marry her first. Richard was proving that he intended doing just that.

'We'll discuss the honeymoon tomorrow,' he told her throatily. 'How does a month in my bedroom sound?'

'Only a month?' she teased, her mouth bare of lipgloss now, although her hair still remained in its sleek chignon, her eyes a luminous gold.

'To start with,' he growled. 'After that I might let you out for short periods of time—as long as you make it up to me when you get back!'

Kate was smiling to herself as she went up to her

flat. Richard had earnt his reputation as the playboy head of James Fashions, a succession of beautiful women passing through his life; she believed him when he said he intended their marriage to be a highly sensual one.

As she searched through her evening bag for her key the door suddenly swung open in front of her. Her startled gaze moved up from the bare feet, the denim-clad legs, the navy blue sweat-shirt and short leather jacket which emphasised the breadth of powerful shoulders. Lastly, the face, the ruggedly handsome face dominated by a roguish smile and laughing blue eyes, thick dark hair falling untidily over his forehead.

Jared's presence in her flat was so unexpected that for a moment Kate was speechless, just stood there staring at him in numbed surprise.

'You'd better come in.' Jared grasped her arm and pulled her inside. 'You look a little strange standing on your own doorstep in that way.'

As the door closed behind them Kate came out of her shock. This was the second time tonight that her door had opened to reveal this man—and this time he was standing on the wrong side of it! 'What are you doing here?' She threw her evening bag down on the side-table, the key superfluous now. 'How did you get in?' she glared at him furiously.

He threw himelf down into one of the armchairs, draping one of his legs over the arm, swinging his bare foot back and forth. 'I told the caretaker I'm your brother,' he told her cheerfully, without regret.

'My *brother*?' she exclaimed in disbelief, her eyes wide gold pools. 'But I don't have a brother!'

'You do now,' he grinned.

'I—You—When I moved into this flat I told the management I don't have any family here in England, least of all a brother——'

'You don't?'

'—and I consider this an invasion of my privacy. Ben had no right to let you in!' she finished with a fierce glare.

'Ben?'

'The caretaker!'

'Oh,' Jared nodded understanding. 'I have to tell you I was very convincing as your relative. I told him all about Great-Aunt Bertha and her recent demise.'

'Geat-Aunt Bertha?' she repeated dazedly. 'But I don't have a Great-Aunt Bertha!'

'I know that,' he laughed. 'But Ben thinks you're going to come into a considerable fortune now that she's dead, that I've come here to tell you all about it. You must realise that he thought you would want to know as soon as possible that you're a rich woman?'

'Don't worry,' her mouth was tight. 'I don't intend making things difficult for Ben, but I will make sure he knows not to let in my long-lost brother again,' she derided. 'Do you realise how awkward this could have been if I'd brought Richard up with me?'

He shrugged. 'I watched out of the window, he drove off as soon as you entered the building.'

Kate sighed her displeasure. 'You have no right to be here. Didn't I make it plain enough earlier this evening, I don't want to see you again?' She was breathing hard in her agitation.

Jared nodded. 'I did seem to detect a certain amount of reluctance on your part. But I had nowhere else to go, and Gill was already otherwise engaged.'

So she had been right about the man in the Lamborghini! 'So that's the reason you came back.' She stood over his chair. 'I don't want you here, Jared. There, is that plain enough for you?' she derided with sarcasm. 'We spent a couple of days together several months ago and you think that allows you to intrude on my life now, to coming into my home like this. Well, let me tell you——'

'Tell me later, Kate,' he encouraged throatily, one hand grasping her wrist as he pulled her easily down into the chair with him. 'God, you're more beautiful than ever,' he groaned before his mouth claimed hers, the pressure of his body above hers forcing her back into the chair.

She didn't want to respond to him, knew that she should push him away, and yet at her first tentative rejection of him her mouth began to part under his, her arms moving up about his neck as her fingers became entangled in the thick dark hair at his nape.

'Beautiful,' he murmured against her throat, slipping the silver jacket from her shoulders to seek out the hollows there, his lips trailing a fire down to the curve of her breasts, his hands on her hips drawing her in to him, telling her of his arousal.

As she gazed down at the dark head below her, felt his lips at her breasts, she knew this was wrong, and she pushed at his chest in earnest now, fighting the languor that was coursing through her body.

'What is it?' Jared looked up at her with bewildered eyes, his sensual arousement obvious in their smoky blue depths. 'What's wrong, darling?' He cupped either side of her face with his long sensitive hands as he searched her face.

'I don't want you here!' Kate managed to struggle up from the chair and stood up, her breasts heaving beneath the black dress in her agitation. 'You see this,' her left hand shook as she held it out to him, the diamond in her ring sparkling its possession. 'This means I belong to another man!'

'Richard James?' His voice was soft, dangerously so, the laughing blue eyes suddenly watchful.

She searched the rugged features warily, suddenly conscious of his change of mood, of the steel in his nature she hadn't even believed possible. So far in their acquaintance Jared had given her the impression that little angered or annoyed him, that he lived a pretty easygoing existence, working when he needed to, not bothering when he didn't, and yet at this moment he did look angry, his eyes narrowed, his nostrils flared, his mouth a taut line, the jaw beneath this rigid with tension.

What right did he have to be angry, what right did he have to be here at all! He was a drifter, a man without ties or commitment, what could he possibly give her, except the same heartache she had known in the past?

'How did you know his name?' she questioned haughtily. 'You didn't know him earlier.'

His mouth twisted as he stood up, his hands thrust into the back pockets of his denims. 'I made the connection later between Richard and Richard *James*. Everyone has heard of him, seen him too. He isn't exactly an elusive figure in the City, is he?' Jared added mockingly.

'Whether he is or isn't is not important, the fact that I wear his ring is,' she snapped.

'Wear it again, don't you mean?' he drawled.

Kate frowned. 'I don't know what you mean . . .'

Jared gave a deep shrug. 'When we met you had an indentation on that finger, as if from wearing a ring. Did you and James fall out, is that the reason you buried yourself in that hotel?'

She turned away. Jared was much more observant than she had given him credit for; she hadn't realised he had noticed that patch of slightly paler skin on her wedding finger. But that hadn't been from wearing Richard's ring, she had accepted that for the first time tonight.

'Well, is he?'

She spun round quickly as she realised how close Jared was standing, and stepped back with a frown. 'No, he isn't, and no, we didn't! My reasons for being at the hotel are none of your business——'

'Then why did you remove his ring?' Jared pursued relentlessly. 'Taking the week off, were you? Having a little affair on the side?'

'No, I wasn't!' Her eyes flashed her indignation. 'Richard and I weren't engaged then.'

Jared clasped her hand, turning it over to look at the thick platinum band. 'No,' he acknowledged softly. 'The mark on your finger was thinner than this ring could have made.' He looked up at her with a frown. 'You wore *another* man's ring here?'

She snatched her hand away, glaring at him. 'I don't have to tell you anything!'

He whistled softly through his even white teeth. 'It *was* another man. Katharine Mary, you surprise me.'

'Why?' Her tone was bitter at the gentle mockery in the deliberately Irish lilt to his voice as he said her name.

'You don't appear to be an indecisive woman, in fact the opposite, and here you are changing fiancés like you would a blouse!'

Kate eyed him with suspicion, but his expression remained deliberately bland. 'Are you laughing at me?' she asked slowly.

He grinned suddenly, one of those wide boyish grins that gave him such a rakish air. 'Whatever gave you that idea?'

Her anger boiled up to gigantic proportions. 'What's so funny about my previous fiancé turning out to be a louse, and the fact that Richard is one of the most powerful and richest men in London?'

'It's an inside joke,' Jared taunted lightly. 'You wouldn't get it at all.'

'I don't!' she snapped.

He shrugged. 'I told you you wouldn't.'

Kate gave an impatient sigh. 'Will you just get out of here,' she said wearily, 'and take your Irish wit with you.'

'Oh, I'm not Irish,' he ignored her first request. 'My father was, but I'm strictly English.'

'In that case you spend little enough time here!' she derided his need to travel.

He nodded. 'I intend changing all that. In fact, I could just decide to settle in one place.'

'I'm sure the social services will be relieved!'

'Hm?' Jared looked puzzled.

'They'll have a permanent address to send your dole money to!'

A smile quirked the firmness of his lips. 'Again you surprise me, Katharine Mary. You were a little abrupt when we first met, but I don't remember you being downright nasty.'

She met his gaze in challenge. 'Well, now you know. And stop calling me Katharine Mary; my name is Kate.'

'To your friends,' he acknowledged. 'I wasn't sure I still came in that category.'

'You don't,' she told him crossly. 'But I haven't been called Katharine since I was at school.'

'I think I prefer it,' he said thoughtfully.

She gave him a saccharine-sweet smile. 'Isn't it a pity your preferences don't interest me!'

He gave a wry laugh. 'I once told you I like your quick mind,' he grimaced. 'But I can tell you now that it's starting to wear a bit thin, with those snide remarks of yours. Perhaps I prefer women without intelligence after all.'

'I'm glad to hear it,' she scorned. 'I'm sure you've had a lot of experience with them. Now if you wouldn't mind, we've been talking for over an hour; I'd like to get to bed.'

'Good idea,' he nodded cheerfully.

'Well?' she prompted as he made no effort to go.

Jared looked puzzled. 'Well what?'

'Shouldn't you be going somewhere too?' she said exasperatedly.

'Oh, don't mind me,' he grinned blandly. 'I'm not sleepy yet. I had a nap on the sofa while you were out—my body clock is still out, you see.'

She didn't give a damn if he hadn't slept for days, she just wanted to get some sleep herself! 'I don't think I'm getting through to you, Jared,' she sighed tautly. 'I want you to leave now—go,' she spoke slowly, clearly, so that there should be no more misunderstandings. 'I want to go to bed.'

'Go?' he repeated in a puzzled voice. 'But where would I go at three o'clock in the morning?'

'I really don't give a damn *where* you go, I just want you to leave!'

He shook his head. 'I can't.'

'*Can't?*'

'Nope,' he confirmed lightly. 'I don't have any money, you see. The job in Canada didn't turn out to be the success I thought it would be, I only just had enough money to get myself back to dear old England.'

'I'll lend you some money to——' He was shaking his head before Kate had even completed her suggestion! 'No?' she rasped tightly.

He continued to shake his head. 'I never take money from a woman.'

'But if I insist . . .'

'I still couldn't do it.' He pursed his lips thoughtfully. 'Besides, what respectable hotel would appreciate my turning up for a room this time of the morning?'

'London doesn't stand on ceremony, you know that. It's a city of transients.'

'Maybe,' he conceded. 'But I'm really quite comfortable where I am.'

And she was far from being comfortable! Jared couldn't possibly stay in her flat overnight. What if Richard should find out?

'I'll leave first thing in the morning, I promise,' Jared seemed to be reading her thoughts. 'You have a spare bedroom, just let me stay here tonight.'

She was beginning to feel too tired to argue any more, with the thought of her full day at the agency looming in front of her. 'All right,' she agreed tautly. 'But you stay in the spare room, and you leave first thing in the morning,' she warningly echoed his words.

'Of course.' He somehow contrived to look hurt. 'Didn't I just say I would?'

'What you say and what you do are two different things,' she bit out.

His eyes darkened, the laughter fading from them for a few minutes. 'Not me, Katharine Mary,' he told her softly. 'I always mean what I say, and I always do it too.'

'A man of his word, hmm?' she sneered with bitterness.

The humour still didn't return. 'I'm sorry you've been hurt, my Katharine,' his voice almost caressed. 'And one day I'd like to hear about the man who did the hurting. Although I realise that right now,' he taunted at the rebellion in her face, 'you would rather tell me to go to hell for daring to intrude into your private pain.'

'You realise right,' she rasped harshly. 'You'll find clean linen in the cupboard in the spare-room,' she added tiredly. 'I trust you know how to make a bed?'

He grinned. 'I already have.'

Kate gave a disbelieving frown, marching over to open the door to her spare bedroom. The bed was neatly made up, the top covers turned back invitingly. She turned to Jared with blazing eyes. 'You were very confident!'

'Not really,' he shook his head. 'I just know my Katharine Mary.'

'You don't know me. And I'm not *your* anything!'

He shrugged. 'I think the answer to both those statements is, not yet.'

'Not ever!'

He sighed. 'Please yourself.'

'I intend to!'

'And I intend pleasing my self too,' he looked at her in challenge. 'And being with you pleases me more than anything else. You really shouldn't have run out on me like you did.'

'I didn't run out on you,' she denied. 'It was time to leave the hotel, so I left.'

'While I was making a telephone call!'

'We had nothing more to say to one another, we'd already said goodbye.'

'Strange,' Jared drawled, 'I don't remember that. I remember asking you to go to North America with me.'

'And I thought you would understand my answer,' she scorned.

'Maybe I did,' he nodded. 'But the Rourkes have never been known to give up.'

For a social drop-out that was a very strange statement! Jared seemed to read her thoughts once again, for his mouth twisted wryly.

'Maybe I just need the right woman to help me settle down,' he said lightly.

Kate's head went back. 'Well, don't look at me!'

'Was I?' he teased.

'You know you were,' she dismissed abruptly. 'But I'm going to marry Richard next month.'

'Of course you are,' Jared nodded.

'Jared?'

He turned, his brows raised in innocent query. 'Hm?'

Kate sighed, putting up a weary hand to her forehead, unconsciously using her left hand, the diamond there sparkling brightly, unknowingly provoking the man standing opposite her.

'Don't worry, me darlin',' once again he spoke with an Irish brogue, pulling her towards him, 'I'm sure the best man will win.'

'Jared, there is *no* contest——'

'Ssh, Katharine Mary,' he spoke into her hair. 'You're too tired tonight to think straight.' He kissed her chastely on the forehead.

'There's nothing to think about!' She pulled away from him, glaring her anger. 'I want you gone from here before I get up in the morning, do you understand?'

Jared looked unperturbed by her vehemence. 'Perfectly. Now don't frown like that,' he advised. 'It'll give you wrinkles.'

With one last exasperated glare she turned and slammed into her bedroom, gritting her teeth to stop herself going back to confront him again as she heard him mutter something about waking the neighbours. They were *her* neighbours, damn it, and she would wake them if she wanted to!

Heavens, she was being ridiculous now! Of course she didn't want to wake the neighbours.

What had she done to bring that tormentor back into her life? It hadn't been her doing at all, if it hadn't been for Brian she would never have been at that hotel in the first place!

She and Brian had met at art college five years ago, and liked each other immediately, spending most of their time together, Kate often cooking for them both in her room. They had fallen into the habit of meeting most evenings, eating a meal together and then spending the rest of the time talking or listening to music. They had been halcyon days, when the future was only as far as tomorrow, and there was still the present to enjoy.

When their college days were over Kate went to work for an advertising agency, not being good enough to become a professional artist herself, but knowing that Brian was. She hadn't minded helping to support him as he struggled to make a name for himself, hadn't cared at all that they rarely went out, or that the engagement ring he had given her on her twenty-first birthday still hadn't been given the accompanying plain gold band even three years later. She understood and respected the fact that Brian wanted to be established in his art before committing himself to marriage.

The time hadn't passed slowly for her. Her own career had progressed very satisfactorily along the path she had chosen, her father helping her out financially when the chance of running her own agency came along. At the time she had considered the longer hours, the hard work, all worthwhile, the money she made after paying her father back his loan helping Brian with his career. She hadn't realised that he resented the fact that she spent less time with him, less time taking care of him, and that he would seek out someone else who could give him the attention he needed.

Coral Simpkins was a rich young widow who had bought one of Brian's paintings from the gallery he submitted them to, her curiosity about the artist making her seek him out. It had been only the first of many meetings, Kate found out months later. Brian had suddenly changed, often being curt with her, and the time between their meetings becoming farther and farther apart. At first she hadn't even noticed that, secure in their love for each other, deeply involved in the advertising agency that had become so much a part of her life. But the night she had finished early at the agency and gone round to surprise Brian had been the night she got *her* surprise!

She had the key to Brian's flat and she let herself in as she usually did, carrying the bottle of wine she had bought to celebrate the success of another contract acquired for her agency. The only light on in the flat had been the one in the studio, but then that wasn't unusual. Brian often worked in there for days at a time without a break. But he hadn't been working that night, and neither had the blonde woman in his arms!

It had been a humiliating as well as a painful experience for Kate, especially as Coral Simpkins felt no awkwardness about the situation. The older woman simply got up from the camp-bed Brian kept in there, pulling on his robe to light a cigarette, looking at Kate insultingly through the smoke.

One thing Coral Simpkins didn't lack was confidence—and she didn't lack Brian at the end of the exchange either. Kate did!

Sorry, Brian said. It just happened, he said. We're in love, he said. We're going to be married, he *said*!

Something had died inside her that night, something precious that she felt sure she would never find again. And she didn't want to find it, not if it meant being disillusioned and hurt by a man she had known and loved for five years. A sensible marriage, with no illusions, to a man who was too sophisticated himself to want a clinging wife, was what she planned for her future, a man who could give her the same power over her own life that he had over his. Richard fitted that role perfectly.

She moved restlessly to get ready for bed, impatient with herself for wasting all this time thinking about Brian when she should have been sleeping. And she *had* been wasting her time, as she had for her five years with him, knew now that he was only interested in what a woman could do for him. And Coral Simpkins—Linton, now—had already done more for him in the two months they had been married than

Kate ever could, Brian's first exhibition being held at a prominent gallery in London. Needless to say, Kate hadn't attended.

A knock sounded on her bedroom door, and she turned sharply, her robe held up in front of her defensively.

Jared came into the room. 'I heard you moving about, so I knew you weren't asleep. I'm just about to make some cocoa, would you like some?'

She stared at him in astonishment. 'It's three-thirty in the morning!'

'I know,' he nodded, not looking in the least tired himself. 'I thought you'd be asleep by now.'

'I——' she shrugged dismissively, evading his searching gaze. 'I'm just about to go to bed now. But help yourself to the cocoa.'

'Thanks,' he accepted lightly, turning to go. 'By the way,' his eyes gleamed with mischief, 'your reflection in the mirror behind you makes the robe superfluous.'

Kate spun round to see herself perfectly reflected in the mirror on her dressing-table, knowing her naked back must have been clearly exposed to Jared as he spoke to her. She turned back to him indignantly, only to find him gone, and sat down heavily on the bed, wondering what had possessed her to let him stay. And yet she had the feeling she hadn't made that decision, that he had made the choice himself. Jared Rourke might be everything that she considered irresponsible, but he seemed to somehow bring things round to his advantage. Well, he would be gone tomorrow, and with luck she would never have to see him again.

The ribbon that had secured her hair while she slept had come loose some time during the night, the long red tresses tangled about her face as she pushed them away impatiently, desperately trying to remember what was causing the feeling of oppression that had been with her as soon as her alarm woke her.

Jared! Of course. Would he have left as they had agreed he should? There was only one way to find out.

She got out of bed, pulling on her robe over her nightgown, quickly brushing the tangles from her hair before going out into the lounge. Jared lay asleep on the sofa, the radio still playing softly where he had fallen asleep with it on. Kate moved to switch it off, watching Jared to see if there were any sign of movement, but there was none. He was still fully dressed, only his short leather jacket removed to reveal the blue sweat-shirt, the long length of his legs stretched over the end of the sofa, too long to fit on it comfortably. He was going to ache all over when he woke up!

When he woke up! That was the problem; he was still here, and he should have been on his way by now. Ben would only have to casually mention to Richard that her 'brother' was staying with her and that would be that. Richard might like to think of himself as sophisticated, but Kate doubted if he would accept another man—a man he would know wasn't her brother!—spending the night with her when *they* had just become engaged.

'Jared!' She deliberately knocked his legs from the arm of the sofa, feeling a moment of regret but knowing the soft approach wouldn't work with this man. Hadn't he somehow persuaded her to let him stay in the first place against her better judgment!

'What—Huh? What's happening . . .?' He came awake with a start, blinking up at her with bloodshot eyes, that and the dark overnight growth of beard on his chin giving him an unkempt look. 'Kate . . .?' He blinked his recognition of her, sitting up to run his long fingers through his hair, its dark thickness falling back into its casually windswept style. 'I'd only just fallen asleep,' he looked up to complain.

'Well, now you can go and sleep somewhere else,' she told him without sympathy. 'I'll be leaving for work in a few minutes and I don't intend that you should still be here when I go.'

'Afraid I might make off with your jewellery?' he mocked.

'Most of what I own isn't worth much,' she assured him. 'The only piece worth having I'm keeping right here,' she held up her left hand.

'You are?' he taunted.

'Yes,' she bit out. 'Now get your things together and leave. It's first thing in the morning, and you made me a promise to be gone then.'

He sat back, looking perfectly relaxed, the sweat-shirt pulled tautly across his chest. 'My morning won't begin until about midnight.'

'The deal was *my* morning——'

'I don't think that was specified——'

'*My* morning, Jared,' she repeated firmly. 'Now I'm going to take a shower and get ready for work. That gives you about twenty minutes.' She went into the bathroom and closed the door, turning the key in the lock for good measure; she didn't trust Jared an inch.

When she came out of the bathroom she could smell coffee being percolated, the fresh aroma filling the flat. Oh well, she had given him twenty minutes, it was up to him how he filled that time. As long as he was gone at the end of it she didn't mind.

Her silky underwear lay in matching sets in her top drawer, the soft lacy bras and panties that she liked to feel against her skin.

'Wear the black,' remarked a husky voice behind her. 'I always liked you in black.'

She spun round, clutching her robe together over

her nakedness. 'Always, Jared?' she mocked to hide her confusion. 'Two days isn't exactly a lifetime.'

He had been leaning against the door-frame, now he moved away from it to walk slowly towards her, his gaze mesmerising. 'It depends who you spend those two days with.'

Kate took a step backwards at the determined glint in his eyes. 'Will you stop this, Jared?' She made her tone sound light. 'We both know we mean nothing to each other.'

'We don't?' He was stalking her now, like a cat stalks its prey.

'No——'

'You mean something to me, Katharine Mary,' he told her softly, very close now, recently washed and shaved, his hair brushed back damply, his shoes and socks back in place.

She moistened her lips. 'I—I do?'

'Yes.' He took her into his arms, moulding her to him to gently claim her lips with his, kissing her with drugging hunger. 'I want you, my darling,' he muttered raggedly against her throat. 'I want you all the time. I haven't been able to get you out of my mind for the last three months. How could I settle to a job in North America when you were all I could think about?' His mouth claimed hers once again, deepening the caress with probing warmth.

'No!' Kate wrenched away from him, fastening the belt of her robe with shaking hands. 'I'm going to marry Richard!'

Jared thrust his hands into his denims pockets, his shoulders hunched over. 'I don't happen to agree with you,' he challenged.

She frowned, swallowing hard as he continued to meet her gaze. The steel was back in his face, and once again she had the fleeting impression that he would make a formidable adversary, although the feeling was only fleeting, instantly dispelled as he grinned once again.

'You see,' he said slowly but clearly, 'I intend marrying you myself.'

CHAPTER THREE

KATE searched the rugged face for signs of madness; there could surely be no other explanation for the outrageous statement he had just made. He just stared straight back at her with clear blue eyes, looking surprisingly boyish despite his thirty-four years.

And why shouldn't he look boyish—the man had probably never taken on a responsibility in the whole of those years! And *she* wasn't about to take on being any man's meal ticket again, even if this one was a charming rogue.

'Do you usually imbibe this time of the morning?' she scorned, turning away.

'Look at me, Kate. Look at me!' Jared repeated harshly as he received no response.

She turned back to him slowly, hardly recognising the 'charming rogue' in this rigid-jawed man. 'I'm looking at you,' she snapped as he made no effort to speak to her.

'And I'm looking at you,' he nodded. 'Not all men are the same as your first fiancé, Kate. Whatever he did to you, I would never do the same.'

'How can you be so sure when you don't even know what he did?' she derided.

'Because I would never do anything to hurt you,' he explained simply.

Her mouth twisted. 'No man will ever be in a position to hurt me again.'

'I just told you——'

'Especially someone like you,' she continued with contempt. 'I've already had a sample of men like you,' she dismissed scornfully, 'and I don't want it again.'

'Men like me?' Jared prompted softly, his stance challenging.

'Yes!' Her eyes flashed deeply gold. 'You drift around the world living from day to day, never giving of yourself but always taking from others. Well, I have nothing to give. I already gave—too damned much,' she added bitterly.

'I want to marry you, Kate,' he bit out tautly.

'And how do you intend to support me?' Her mouth turned back with scorn. 'Or didn't that enter into the plan of things? Of course it didn't,' she derided. 'You like an independent woman—now I realise why. I don't intend marrying you, Jared. I met you at a time when I was feeling vulnerable, bruised, in need of someone to help me through a difficult experience in my life. But as far as I'm concerned that's all there was to it. I'm sorry if you read more into it than what there was.'

'Are you?' he rasped.

She sighed heavily. 'Look, Jared, at the time I needed you. You had a sleeping partner for a couple of days and I managed to sort out my life, that's all there was to it,' she dismissed again. 'We didn't make any vows or lasting commitments to each other. It was a physical interlude, nothing else.' And it was an interlude that would probably haunt her for the rest of her life, completely out of character for her, although she wasn't going to tell him that; better that he continued to think of her as a sophisticate.

Jared looked at her wordlessly for several long seconds. 'So the idea of marriage to me doesn't appeal to you?' he finally drawled.

She shook her head. 'Not in the least.'

He shrugged. 'You're honest anyway. I suppose Richard James is a better prospect, isn't he? He's rich and socially acceptable——'

'Jared, please, I didn't mean it that way——'

'Didn't you?' His brows rose. 'You'll have to forgive me, but it sounded that way.'

She knew it did, and if she was honest with herself she knew it was the way she felt. Jared was another Brian, would drain her of everything she had emotionally and financially if she let him. And she wasn't going to do that. Richard could give her everything she would ever need, and in return she would make him a good wife, a good social hostess.

Marrying Jared was out of the question; she didn't love him, and he certainly didn't love her. She couldn't imagine what had prompted his proposal.

'I have to get ready for work now.' She didn't pursue the subject of marriage between them, knowing that anything else she said would only sound more insulting. Much as she wanted Jared out of her life, she didn't want to hurt him.

'And I have to be on my way,' he nodded abruptly.

'Jared . . .!' she stopped him at the bedroom door.

His eyes were narrowed as he looked over at her. 'Yes?'

Kate felt guilty for taking the humour out of his eyes, but as she knew from her experience with Brian, any sign of weakness on her part and Jared would never leave. 'Do you need any money for a hotel? I have some I——'

'You're far from the only person I know in London, Kate,' he bit out harshly.

She flushed at the rebuke. 'I didn't think I was. I'm sorry if I sounded——'

'Patronising?' he finished softly. 'You did, but I can take it. We spongers on society get used to the abuse after a while.'

'Jared!' she said appealingly.

'Okay,' he sighed dismissively. 'I should learn to take a refusal to a marriage proposal in a more gentlemanly fashion. Only I think you've just finished telling me I'd never qualify for the title!'

She chewed on her bottom lip, knowing she deserved his anger. But she couldn't take back a word she had said, not when it was the way she really felt.

'I'll be seeing you, Kate.' Once again the affectionate 'Katharine Mary' had been dropped, his derision for her clearly visible in flinty blue eyes. 'One day you're going to realise there's a whole lot more to life than diamond rings and Porsches,' he told her curtly. 'And I hope it's before you marry Richard James. Otherwise you're going to make life very difficult for yourself.'

'I'll manage,' she scorned.

'I hope so. I doubt if Richard James will understand if you take a couple of days off with a lover to "find yourself" once you're married to him!'

'It wasn't like that——'

'It sounds that way to me!' he told her contemptuously. 'I'll be seeing you, Kate.' He turned on his heel and left the room, the door slamming forcefully behind him.

Kate felt a little breathless from the exchange, and sat down on the edge of the bed, jumping nervously as she heard the flat door closing several seconds later, more gently this time, as if some of the quick temper had already started to leave him. While it lasted it had been formidable, but once his anger faded Jared would be back to his carefree self, would forget he had ever proposed to a redhead called Katharine Mary Collier.

As she had forgotten him an hour later, her mind completely engrossed in her agency, as it had been from the beginning when she was struggling to make a success of it, having half a dozen people working for her now, all top professionals who gave her and their clients exactly what was needed.

She had an appointment herself with one of the directors of a high-class furniture warehouse at ten o'clock, and was just in the middle of explaining the details of the new season's advertising when the telephone on her desk rang. She frowned, having told Beryl, her secretary, not to put any calls through while she was in this meeting.

'It's Colin Harkness,' Beryl explained pointedly.

The advertising executive she had been dealing with at Melfords! She glanced frustratedly at Charles Denison as he sat across the desk from her, longing to take the call and yet knowing 'a client on the books was worth a dozen prospective ones'. 'Could you take a message, Beryl?' she requested with a confidence she was far from feeling. 'Or ask if I might return his call later?'

'Will do.' Beryl sounded totally bemused by the fact that Kate was unable to take the call she had been waiting for for weeks. Colin Harkness had proved to be an elusive man when she had tried to contact him the past few weeks, always being in conference or not in the office at all.

But what could she do? She couldn't exactly walk out on Charles Denison in the middle of a meeting to take the call in the outer office, and there was no question of her taking it in here in front of him. Each client's work was confidential, and a possible client like Melfords wouldn't even like it known that they had contacted her, several other advertising agencies being interested in their contract.

The time she spent with Charles Denison seemed to drag, and Beryl did not get back to her about the Harkness call. But Kate was a professional, and she made no attempt to hurry Charles out of her office. Here in this building, in this office, was where she lived and breathed, and she had been glad of its prop in the weeks following Brian's defection.

But finally Charles stood up to leave, and she walked out with him to the door, her smile replaced by a frown as she hurried back to Beryl's desk to find out what Colin Harkness's reaction had been to her message.

'He said he would call you back when he had the time,' Beryl sympathised; she was a woman in her early thirties with a bubbly personality that somehow managed to combine a family of a husband and three children with a career.

'Damn!' Kate muttered, chewing the end of her pen. 'We both know what that means.'

'Hm,' Beryl grimaced. 'It's taken him almost a month to return this call.' She monitored all the calls that came through to the office on her switchboard.

'Yes,' Kate still frowned. 'And if I call him back I'll probably get his shrewish secretary again.'

'Probably,' the other woman nodded. 'I—What on earth——!' She was staring past Kate to the glass doors at the entrance.

Kate turned to see a huge bouquet of red roses advancing down the open-plan office towards her, the person carrying them obscured completely; there must be dozens of roses there. 'Have you and Tom had a fight?' she murmured dazedly to Beryl.

'Not that I know of,' Beryl muttered. 'And even if we had he wouldn't spend a fortune on roses—he knows I would kill him!'

Kate smiled, wondering how the man laden down with the bouquet could see where he was going. She had never seen so many roses!

'Delivery for Miss Collier,' the man spoke gruffly to Beryl.

Kate gave a start of surprise. For her? But— Richard! He must have sent them as another celebration of their engagement. She knew he was a generous man, but this was ridiculous! 'I'm Miss Collier. I——' she froze as the roses were lowered and twinkling blue eyes looked back at her with laughter.

Jared! She knew she must have paled, blinking dazedly. What on earth was he doing here?

Whatever it was he was once again making things awkward for her, everyone at the agency aware that her engagement to Richard had been announced yesterday. If she acknowledged Jared now it would arouse speculation as to where he came into her life.

'Would you like me to take them through to your office, Miss Collier?' he enquired politely—almost as if he really were someone from the florist's making a delivery to a complete stranger!

'Er—yes. Yes—thank you,' she added awkwardly, following him to close the door behind them, her voice lowered because of the thinness of the walls between her office and the large outer one. 'What are you doing here?' she demanded agitatedly, looking nothing like the cool young woman in the black and white business suit who had dealt so efficiently with Charles Denison minutes earlier, having a decidedly harassed look about her now.

'Delivering roses.' He held up the bouquet pointedly.

'But why? Have you got a job in a florists——'

'There's a card somewhere.' He searched the cellophane covering for the small white envelope that accompanied the roses. 'Mind if I sit down?' He did so, putting the roses down on her desk—covering most of it—before handing her the envelope.

Kate ripped the flap open and read the single word written there, 'Sorry'. She looked up at Jared with a frown. 'But who sent them?'

He arched dark brows. 'Guess.'

'You . . .?'

He grinned. 'I told you I like intelligent women.'

'You later rescinded that statement,' she reminded him in a preoccupied voice, looking from him to the roses and then back again, unconsciously noting his

masculine grace in the tight denims and thick cream
sweater he now wore, obviously having been somewhere to change since leaving her flat this morning.
And to get the roses. 'How did you——'

'Pay for them?' he finished lightly as she seemed to
falter. 'With money, how else?'

'But where . . .?'

'It should be on the lunchtime news,' he drawled. 'I
robbed a bank!'

'Very funny!' She sat down opposite him. 'Where
did you really get the money, Jared?'

He shrugged. 'You shouldn't always judge by
appearances, they can sometimes be deceptive. I could
be an eccentric millionaire who just likes drifting
around the world.'

Her mouth twisted at the thought. 'And I could be
Brigitte Bardot!'

'No, you couldn't,' he shook his head. 'You don't
have the French accent. You have everything else,
though,' and he gave her a lecherous look.

She gave an impatient sigh; she was not in the mood
for his humour right now. 'You still haven't answered
my question.'

'Because you had no right to ask it,' he rebuked
gently. 'I wanted to apologise for my bad temper this
morning, I thought the roses might help you forgive
me. Where they came from, or how I paid for them,
isn't important.'

'I think the bad temper was a two-sided thing,' she
smiled.

The laughter returned to his eyes as he saw her
mood lighten. 'In that case you can pay for half the
roses!'

'Typical!' she grimaced. 'Couldn't you take them
back?' she joined in his lighthearted teasing.

'I don't think so,' he shook his head. 'They don't
usually sell roses on approval.'

Kate smiled. 'Well, they're very welcome, thank you. Although I'll have to leave them here,' she frowned as she realised that.

'Your fiancé,' he nodded, perfectly relaxed, his arms folded across his chest.

'Mm.'

'Was he the reason you were looking so pensive when I arrived?' Jared raised dark brows.

'No.' Her thoughts turned once again to the call from Colin Harkness that she had had to miss. 'Just a prospective client,' she dismissed.

'Denison?'

'How did you know about him?' she gasped her surprise.

'I saw him leave,' Jared shrugged. 'I told you, I know a few people in the business world,' he answered her next question. 'He's a client of yours, isn't he?'

'It's no secret,' she confirmed.

'Then it isn't him that's bothering you,' he murmured thoughtfully. 'Prospective, you said. And someone important, by the look of you——'

'Were you a dectective in a previous life?' she derided.

'Couldn't I be one now?' he mocked.

She gave him a considering look, meeting laughing blue eyes, the lines beside his eyes and the grooves in his cheeks made from laughter too. 'No,' she smiled. 'You don't look sinister enough.'

'I don't?' he laughed. 'I know a few people who wouldn't agree with you.' He sat forward, picking up her notepad from the desk. 'Interesting doodles, Katharine Mary,' he studied the squiggles and drawings on the pad. 'A psychiatrist would have a lot of fun with your inner mind, my darling,' he teased. 'Colin Harkness,' he read slowly. 'Now what would you be doing writing down the name of the advertising executive of Melfords?' He quirked dark brows questioningly.

Kate snatched her pad out of his hand, not even aware that she had written Colin Harkness's name down until Jared pointed it out to her. 'Are you a spy?' she snapped impatiently.

'No.' He studied her flushed face. 'Are Melfords the prospective client?'

'Jared, really! I——'

'I know you can't really tell me that,' he reassured her. 'But it would seem to make sense. It would be a definite feather in your cap, wouldn't it?'

'Yes, I—— Are you sure you aren't a spy?' she groaned her chagrin. 'I should never have told you anything about it!'

'Now who am I likely to tell?'

'One of your seemingly endless contacts in the business world!'

'My lips are sealed!' He sobered suddenly. 'Seriously, Kate, whatever you tell me is in the strictest confidence.'

She believed him. There was a sincerity in his voice and face that told her she could trust him. She sighed. 'You're right, I am trying for Melfords, although Harkness is proving difficult to contact, and Richard——' she broke off, realising she was being disloyal discussing Richard with this man. She stood up to sit on the front of her desk to cover the moment of awkwardness. 'They're a big company,' she amended brightly. 'I'm probably being over-ambitious.'

'Is that what Richard thinks?' Jared taunted.

Her eyes flashed deeply gold. 'Did you come here to have another argument?'

He held up his hand. 'I came only to apologise, to tell you I was being unfair to you this morning. I have no right to propose to you when you've only just become engaged to someone else.'

Kate smiled. 'I knew you would regret it once you had had time to think about it. Don't worry, Jared, I don't intend holding you to your proposal.'

'No?' He stood up, walking to the door. 'That's a pity—because I have no intention of letting you marry anyone else but me.'

'Jared——' Too late, he had opened the door, and with a wicked wink in Beryl's direction as he passed her desk, he had gone.

Kate gave a sigh of frustration, then stood up to close her office door. As she turned the roses caught her eye. She was never going to be able to find enough vases for them all; there must be at least six dozen here!

Beryl tapped on her office door, coming in after a slight pause. 'Need any help with the flowers?' she offered.

Kate picked up the whole bouquet and put it into her secretary's arms. 'Could you put them into vases, please. If you don't have enough then go out and buy some more. Oh, and Beryl,' she stopped the other woman on her way out of the door, 'I don't want any of them in my office.'

'But——'

'I'm allergic,' she invented, turning away before she changed her mind.

With a slightly puzzled frown Beryl went back into her own office. And Kate knew the reason for the other woman's puzzlement; she had never been allergic to anything in her life, let alone beautiful deep red roses! But she didn't want one single reminder of Jared in her office, wanted to forget about him and his wild statements. No man could force her into marrying him. Then why did this uneasy feeling inside her persist?

The call back from Colin Harkness later that

afternoon really wasn't expected; Kate had not exactly been getting co-operation from him in the past. She had been expecting at least another week or so's wait from him again. The suggestion that she go in and see him to discuss her ideas was even more of a shock.

'Wh-when?' she gasped, feeling as if she had just been granted an audience with a member of royalty.

'At your convenience,' the man said haughtily.

'At my——? Er—yes, of course.' Her composure was completely thrown, her thoughts racing. She was tempted to say she was free right now, that she would come over immediately, before he changed his mind, but that would have seemed very unprofessional. Besides, that seemed to be the reaction he expected.'I could be free tomorrow some time,' she told him coolly. 'I'll just check my diary. Ah yes,' she said after a suitable pause, 'I have a free hour between eleven and twelve, is that convenient for you?'

'Of course, Miss Collier. I'm sure you know it is,' he added almost resentfully.

She frowned. 'I——'

'I'll expect you at eleven o'clock tomorrow,' he cut in abruptly. 'Please endeavour not to be late.' He rang off.

Kate put down her own receiver more slowly. Colin Harkness had agreed to see her, but it seemed almost as if he did it under protest. Which was ridiculous! Maybe he was always this curt with people, his position of power in Melfords certainly gave him the opportunity to be.

'I've never met the man, Kate,' Richard told her that evening when she asked him about Colin Harkness. 'Melfords may be a successful company, but they do it without much publicity to themselves, personally.' He shrugged. 'Harkness is known as a powerful man in the company, that's all I know about him. Darling, I thought we were going to discuss the wedding and our honeymoon this evening?' He looked irritated by her talk of business.

Kate bit back the urge to discuss Melfords with him further, knowing that when he was with her he disliked talking about her business; though James Fashions was a different matter entirely! But she had known that before she agreed to marry him, had known it and accepted it. She couldn't have everything in her marriage; a young and attractive husband, rich and influential, was more than enough.

'Of course we are, darling.' She sat down to curl herself against his side. 'It's high on my list of priorities.'

But not as high as the contract with Melfords, and it was still very much on her mind as she closed the door on Richard after having said goodnight to him a couple of hours later, with the wedding date decided on a month hence, their honeymoon to be spent in romantic France.

When the doorbell rang a few minutes later she didn't need two guesses as to who it was. Only Jared would have the nerve to call on someone at eleven-thirty at night!

Kate wrenched the door open, her anger fading as she saw the hopeful smile on his lips. He had his rucksack thrown over one shoulder, his suitcase in his other hand.

'I spent my hotel money on roses for a beautiful lady,' he told her ruefully, as she made no effort to speak to him but simply stared at him wordlessly.

Her mouth firmed. 'In that case, the "beautiful lady" will reimburse you.'

Jared shook his head. 'I told you, I never take money from a woman.'

'Then what do you want?'

He shrugged. 'The use of the bed I never quite got to last night.'

Kate gave an impatient sigh. 'My fiancé has just left——'

'I know,' he nodded. 'I watched him go.'

'I might have guessed!'

He grinned. 'I wouldn't dream of interrupting your evening.'

'Just asking for the use of my spare bedroom,' she drawled.

He gave a rueful shrug. 'It will only be for tonight. I'll find somewhere else for tomorrow.'

Her mouth twisted. 'I seem to remember an angry man telling me this morning that he knew plenty of people in London.'

'And I do,' he told her. 'But most of the friends I tried today are either living with someone or they need the privacy to seduce their lady. I didn't think you would mind.'

'Really?' Her tone was dry.

'You do?' he grimaced.

'Because of you Ben seems to think I'm going to become an heiress any day now,' she scowled. 'It took me ten minutes to get away from his good wishes this evening.'

Jared look unperturbed. 'He was pleased for you.'

'So would I be if it were true!'

'Never mind, Katharine Mary,' he walked past her into the flat, 'you're engaged to a rich man, you'll soon have a rich husband.'

She closed the door and followed him through to the lounge, watching as he put the case and rucksack on the floor. 'You can't stay here, you know,' she told him.

He frowned. 'Why not?'

'Because——'

'Of propriety?' he finished lightly, shrugging. 'I've never much cared for that myself. As long as I don't intentionally hurt anyone, and what I do isn't illegal, I don't see the use of convention *or* propriety.' He sat down on the sofa, his long legs stretched out in front of him, the denims he wore tonight even more disreputable and patched, his shirt dark blue, the black leather jacket fitting him comfortably. 'Do you?'

Kate sighed at his philosophy on life; it might be a good one, but it wasn't practical. 'Richard wouldn't like you staying here.'

'And your other fiancé,' he looked up at her curiously. 'What did he like? Did he used to stay here with you himself?'

The colour entered her cheeks against her will. 'That's none of your business!'

'He did,' Jared nodded his head. 'I knew I wasn't the first with you, but you aren't very experienced either, are you?' He eyed her challengingly.

'Jared——'

'You aren't fooling anyone, Katharine Mary,' he gently rebuked. 'And sleeping with your ex-fiancé is nothing to be ashamed of. I'm sure you loved him at the time.'

'I may have done——'

'I know you did,' he told her confidently. 'But you don't love him now. What happened, Kate? You once told me he was a louse, what did he do to you?' He frowned up at her with serious intensity. 'I need to know,' he added softly.

He didn't *need* to know anything about her! How dared he come here and assure her that she had nothing to be ashamed of because she had made love with Brian—*he* was the one she was ashamed of going to bed with! 'Why?' she snapped. 'So you don't make the same mistake?'

'I thought I'd already made it,' he derided at her sarcasm. 'I'm poor, and I want to marry you.'

She gave an uncomfortable blush. 'Brian's problem didn't lie in either of those things,' she told him tightly. 'As yours doesn't. The reason I can't even think about marrying you is that I've agreed to marry Richard. I didn't marry Brian because he decided to marry someone else.'

Jared's eyes narrowed. 'And what did you decide, to marry a man who could take care of you for a change, who could give you the support *you* need?'

Her blush deepened at his shrewdness. 'Richard will make me a good husband,' she nodded acknowledgment.

'But will you make him a good wife?'

'Yes!' Her eyes flashed deeply gold.

'I believe you,' he drawled. 'Tell me about your last fiancé.'

Kate turned away. 'I've already told you about him—he married someone else. Look, I'm tired, Jared. I had a late night last night, and it's been a long day today. I think I'll go to bed.'

He stood up, suddenly forceful, the impression of a sleeping tiger dispersed. 'No!' He relaxed with effort. 'Why don't you have a shower, it will ease away the tension of the day. I'll make us both some coffee.'

'Do I take that to mean you intend staying?'

'Do I?' He quirked dark brows.

She gave a sigh of defeat. 'For tonight,' she agreed wearily. 'But you really can't make a habit of it,' she added warningly.

'I won't.' He was already on his way to the kitchen to make the coffee.

Kate gave a shrug of acceptance, too tired to argue any more tonight, and she had the interview with Colin Harkness to think about without worrying about Jared making use of her spare bedroom.

The shower did a lot to refresh her, and the smell of newly percolated coffee coming from the kitchen made her feel even better. The supper of cheese sandwiches Jared had also prepared came as a complete surprise.

'You don't eat enough,' he talked down her objection as she protested when he insisted she eat some of the sandwiches.

'Cheese last thing at night gives me nightmares,' she defended, her black silk robe secured tightly over her black lace nightdress, her hair brushed into a silky curtain and secured at her nape like a copper flame.

His mouth twisted. 'If that happens I'll be only too glad to come and wake you up, to—comfort you,' he taunted, the leather jacket discarded, the sleeves of the navy blue shirt turned back to just below his elbows, revealing the dark hair that covered his tanned skin, his arms strong and muscled, as was the rest of his body.

'I'm sure you will,' Kate returned dryly, sitting on one of the stools at the breakfast bar, enjoying the aromatic coffee. 'But I'm sure I won't need comforting.'

'Pity,' he shrugged nonchalantly, pushing the plate of sandwiches at her and sitting at her side. 'So why did Brian marry someone else?' He looked at her challengingly.

She gave an impatient sigh and slammed her cup down, having thought the subject forgotten. 'Jared——'

'Is it a secret?' he mocked. 'Did you pull one of your "I want to be alone" stunts and he just got tired of waiting for you to come back?'

'No, I didn't!' She stood up, breathing deeply. 'I fell in love with Brian when I was nineteen, I loved him for five years, I thought he felt the same way about me——' Once she had begun talking she couldn't stop, the words coming out of her mouth heatedly, not stopping until she had told Jared everything about her engagement to Brian, and the traumatic way it had ended. 'He and Coral have been married for a couple of months now,' she finished dully.

'Why didn't you fight for him?'

She turned to Jared with fierce eyes. 'What was there to fight for? He'd already made his choice!'

'So couldn't you have tried to change his mind?'

Her mouth tightened. 'No.'

'You didn't want to.'

'I didn't need to!' Once again her eyes flashed. 'Brian had decided there was room for both Coral and me in his life, Coral as his rich wife, I as his—his mistress,' her mouth tightened with distaste. 'His decision wasn't acceptable to me.'

'Nor to me,' Jared bit out. 'I would have killed him if he'd forced you into that role.'

Kate gave a tight smile. 'If he hadn't made the suggestion I wouldn't have needed to get away, and then the two of us would never have met.'

'We would,' he nodded. 'Some things are meant to be. And I've been searching for you for thirty-four years.'

'Fate, Jared?' she queried.

'That's one word for it.'

'Then my fate is to marry Richard.' She took her empty cup over to the sink, and rinsed out the cup. 'And yours is to find yourself a job,' she mocked gently.

'There's no hurry,' he shrugged.

'I don't intend being your hotel for more than this one night,' seriousness underlined her tone this time. 'You do realise that?'

'I realise,' he nodded. 'Don't worry, a friend of mine has a bed I can use tomorrow.'

'Female?' Her voice sharpened.

His mouth quirked mockingly. 'And if it is?'

She shrugged. 'I was just curious.'

'It's a male friend,' he smiled. 'He's going out of town for a few days and said I could use his flat while he's away. Unfortunately he needed his privacy tonight, to say goodbye to his lady. Have a sandwich, Katharine Mary.' Once again he pushed the plate of sandwiches towards her, helping himself to one, biting into it hungrily. 'I didn't have any dinner,' he explained at her raised brows.

'Help yourself.' Kate yawned tiredly. 'I'll see you in the morning.' She found herself blushing at how intimate that sounded. 'Er—goodnight.'

Jared stood up slowly, his gaze holding hers as he pulled her determinedly towards him. 'Goodnight, my darling,' he murmured before capturing her mouth with his, his lips moving druggingly against hers in a passion that was devouring.

Her body arched against his without volition, her arms up about his neck as she kissed him back, feeling her senses swim, falling under the same magic she had known with him three months ago.

His hands moved deftly to the tie of her belt, releasing it to slip the robe softly from her shoulders to the floor, leaving her in only the clinging black lace nightgown, the sheer cups clearly showing the rose tips to her breasts, the taut nipples thrusting against Jared's chest.

'Kate . . .!' he groaned raggedly. 'Marry me, Kate. Marry me and we can be together like this for the rest of our lives.' His mouth moved sensuously against her throat as one of his hands caressed beneath the lacy top of her nightgown, cupping her breast with a familiarity that made her tremble.

Pleasure quivered through her body as his thumbtip caressed the hardened nipple, weakness in her legs at the intimacy making her cling to him, her fingers curling into the taut muscles of his shoulder.

'Kate?' he prompted huskily. 'Will you marry me?'

She stiffened in his arms, not wanting to talk, but knowing she had to listen to herself as well as Jared. She pulled back to look up at him, meeting darkened blue eyes, his face taut with tension. And the tension was because of her lack of an answer to his proposal. But she had given him her answer this morning, and she wasn't going to change her mind even if he had tried to seduce her into doing exactly that.

She bent to pick up her robe, slipping it on easily, trying her belt with fluid movements. 'My answer is still no, Jared,' she told him calmly. 'Could you just tidy up in here before you go to bed?' She walked to the door. 'I expect to be leaving early in the morning, so I don't have time to clean up after you.'

Jared seemed to be a little longer regaining his equilibrium, although he was soon smiling, shrugging off his tension of a few minutes ago with a nonchalance that belied the steel in his eyes. 'What are you going to do when I stop asking?' he mocked.

'*Thank* you!' Kate was smiling lightly as she left the room, although that faded as soon as she reached her bedroom, leaving her leaning weakly back against the door.

What was *wrong* with her? She had been taken in by a man like Jared once—and she had almost done it again!

What she had told Jared about Brian had been the truth; he had wanted her to become his mistress, had claimed he couldn't lose her, that she meant too much to him to go out of his life completely.

She had left Brian's flat that night feeling totally shattered after seeing him with Coral, her tears of bitterness and pain taking her through to the morning. Brian had been the last person she had expected to see when she answered the door later that day. He wanted nothing to change between them, assured her that Coral wouldn't interfere in their own relationship. Kate hadn't known him in that moment, had decided she had never known him—and that she didn't particularly want to any more.

She had loved him and he had betrayed her, and she had a feeling Jared could induce the same weakening emotion in her. And that he would one day hurt her just as much as Brian had, whereas Richard taking a mistress wouldn't hurt her at all, in fact she half expected it after the initial period of their marriage.

The thought of marrying Jared and having him treat her as Brian had was unpalatable to her—and she refused to even allow herself to think why it was. She *wasn't* marrying him, and that was the end of the matter.

CHAPTER FOUR

THE oppression Kate had felt on waking the previous morning wasn't with her today, and she knew that part of the reason for that was the mouthwatering smell of bacon cooking that was wafting through the flat. Having an unwelcome guest seemed to have some advantages!

She stretched languorously and threw back the bedclothes, and was just in the process of putting her feet into the fluffy black mule slippers when her bedroom door opened without warning.

'Oh, you're awake,' Jared grinned from the doorway, black cords moulded to his thighs and long legs, a yellow tee-shirt fitted to his chest and shoulders. 'That's a shame—I was hoping I could kiss you awake. And I'm very disappointed the nightmare didn't materialise, but maybe another night . . .? No?' he grimaced at the shake of her head. 'Oh well . . . Do you prefer your breakfast in bed or out of it?'

Kate straightened in her sitting position on the edge of the bed. 'Out of it. Just as I prefer *you* out of my bedroom!'

He raised mocking eyebrows. 'I'm hungry for bacon right now, not you. It will be on the table in five minutes, is that long enough for you?'

'I suppose it will have to be,' she nodded, determined not to let him know how good she had found it to wake up and find him here. This could become habit-forming!

So could this constant self-recrimination. She couldn't dictate Jared's movements, and if he chose to haunt her apartment, let him. He would soon tire of it when he realised it was getting him nowhere. And in the meantime it was very nice to wake up and find her breakfast cooked for her.

'What's the rush?' Jared frowned as he watched her hurry over the breakfast of fresh orange juice, eggs and bacon, and toast he had prepared for her.

'I told you last night.' She looked up from gulping down her coffee, conscious of the passing of the minutes. 'I have to leave early; I have an important appointment.'

'When?'

'Eleven. And I——'

'But it's only eight o'clock,' he frowned.

'And I have to prepare for it. The appointment was made late yesterday afternoon, and as I had a date with Richard last night that didn't give me the time I need to get ready.'

'I'm sure you're always prepared. Your agency has a very good reputation.'

She eyed him curiously. 'Your friend in advertising?'

'That's right,' he mocked. 'So who's the lucky man?'

'Man?' Kate raised her brows. 'I don't remember mentioning that my appointment was with a man.'

'My detective instincts again,' he told her, his eyes twinkling with humour. 'You would hardly dress that way,' he looked appreciatively at the femininely fitted green suit and tailored paler green blouse, her hair in a neat coil at her nape, drawing attention to the riveting beauty of her high-cheekboned face, 'for another woman,' he drawled.

'Now that's where you're wrong.' Her mouth twisted with humour. 'I've been known to dress my very best for female clients. It always helps to feel confident over another woman.'

'I would have thought it more successful business

practice to play down your own attraction,' he taunted. 'To give her the upper hand, so to speak.'

'Not in my profession. Clients demand—and expect, glamour and polish in advertising,' she explained. 'And they have to see that visual effect projected from me first.'

Jared gave a nod of appreciative acknowledgment. 'You certainly know your business; you project glamour and polish today. Let's hope the man in question isn't past appreciating such loveliness.'

A frown darkened the golden almond of her eyes. 'Do you think he might be?' she voiced her sudden uncertainty. 'You seem to know Colin Harkness——'

'*Of* him,' Jared corrected softly.

Kate nodded impatiently. 'Well, what do you know of him? I talked to Richard and he said that Melfords as a whole keeps to itself. I usually like to know a little about the people I'm to meet.' Her frown returned.

'And Colin Harkness is the man you're going to see this morning?'

She flushed her guilt at revealing so much. 'Yes.'

'Then James is right, Melfords are a very private company.' He was suddenly serious. 'Harkness is a bit of a cold fish, very correct. Your beautiful body in that very attractive suit won't mean a thing to him,' he said with regret, his own gaze still appreciative.

'Oh.'

'But maybe your mind will.' He sensed her disappointment. 'Harkness has a reputation for being dour, but even he doesn't turn away real talent. And I'm sure you have that.'

'I wish I had your confidence,' Kate grimaced.

'You have,' he reassured her, his hand covering hers as it rested on the table. 'And it will all come back to you when you face Harkness. *I* have confidence in you.'

She gave him a startled look. 'You do?'

'I do,' he nodded, smiling encouragement. 'You can do it, Katharine Mary.'

As she looked into the depths of laughing blue eyes she really felt as if she could indeed go into Colin Harkness's office and convince him she was capable of handling the multi-million-pound company's contract.

'Come on.' Jared stood up, holding out her jacket for her. 'Go out there and impress him with your expertise.'

She felt caught up in his enthusiasm, feeling a surge of self-confidence that had slowly been waning since Colin Harkness's call yesterday afternoon.

'Handbag, madam.' Jared handed her the black leather clutch-bag that matched her shoes in colour.

'Thank you,' she laughed lightly, tucking the bag under her arm. 'Will I do?' She did a light twirl on her high heels.

'More than that,' he growled as he took her into his arms. 'I'm afraid your lip-gloss is going to need renewing,' he murmured before his lips gently claimed hers. He was smiling as he stepped back from her, aware of her capitulation to the light caress. 'I won't wish you good luck,' he touched one of her flushed cheeks. 'You don't need it.'

Kate forgot all about the bareness of her lips, still filled with the confidence he had given her as she drove to work. If only Richard could have given her the same support—No, she wouldn't compare the two men! Why not? Because already Richard came out unfavourably? No, of course not, she denied fiercely to herself. Jared had nothing to lose by encouraging her career, Richard wanted a wife, not a business-woman. She wouldn't compare the two men again!

Colin Harkness was everything she had expected and more! Jared had described the man as dour; to Kate he looked downright bad-tempered and ominous. A man of about fifty, with iron-grey hair, flinty grey eyes and a thin ramrod-straight body, he hardly seemed the sort of man who would be connected with a perfume empire—in any capacity.

On the wide mahogany desk in front of him was the file with the ideas she had sent him for advertising a new line in men's colognes and after-shaves two months ago. He opened the file with a disdainful flick of his wrist. 'Some of your ideas are in line with the new image we have planned for the company——'

'I'm glad to hear it. I——'

'And some of them are totally unsuitable.' He closed the file with a decisive thud, leaning forward on his arms to look at her with icy grey eyes. 'I saw you today because——' he broke off as the telephone on his desk began to ring, looking down at it irritably. 'Excuse me,' he rasped, picking up the receiver.

Kate turned away politely as he reprimanded his secretary for putting the call through when he had told her not to interrupt him for any reason, although her interest deepened as his manner changed as he listened to his secretary's reply.

'But—Yes,' he was obviously talking to his caller now, someone who meritted his grudging respect. 'Yes, sir,' he glanced at Kate with venomous eyes. 'Of course. Yes, I'll see to it. I——' He glared furiously at the receiver as his caller rang off, slamming it down angrily.

Kate could see he was livid with anger, and she feared for the meeting that had already shown signs of deterioration into becoming a complete rejection of her agency and her. So much for Jared's confidence in her intelligence—she hadn't even had time to convince him of the merit of the agency's work! Any second now he was going to dismiss her and forget he had ever agreed to see one Kate Collier.

Once again the file was flicked open and several

sheets pushed across the desk at her. 'These are the ideas we would like you to expand on,' Colin Harkness bit out harshly. 'The rest,' he pushed the file towards her, 'you can dispose of.'

Kate still had the impression that this man despised her, that she could be exactly what this company needed and he would still want to turn her down. Something—or someone—was compelling him to at least consider her and her agency.

She stood up with a haughty frown at the man across the desk from her. 'I never dispose of any of my work, Mr Harkness,' she told him coolly. 'And I can see you aren't really interested in any of the ideas I proposed——'

'I didn't say that, Miss Collier.' The man gave an ingratiating smile as he stood up, deep lines grooved into his austere features, as if smiling didn't come naturally to him. 'Of course we're interested in all your work.'

'You didn't give that impression a few minutes ago,' she frowned, as a sudden thought occurred to her, one she didn't like in the least. 'Did who my fiancé is have anything to do with your change of mind?' After all, Richard was an important man in the City, and this man was probably as capable as the next person of being influenced by such things. 'To making you decide to see me at all?'

Colin Harkness seemed to visibly pale. 'Your fiancé . . .?'

'Yes,' she bit out. 'Because if it did I would rather you forgot about it for the moment. He has nothing to do with my trying to get this contract with you.' It hadn't occurred to her that Richard's influence in the business world would interfere in her own career, having expected that his money and power would only affect her in a private way. Which was ridiculous, if this man's reaction was anything to go by; he was almost frothing at the mouth in an effort to stop her leaving!

His gaze seemed to be fixed on the engagement ring on her finger, as if he had just noticed it. 'Er—you've set a date for the wedding?'

She flashed him an irritated frown. 'Next month,' she dismissed.

'I had no idea . . .' The man was visibly shaken.

'I can assure you it will not affect my working for you—if you decide to give me the contract,' Kate added stiffly.

'No, of course not.' The mouth smiled but the eyes remained flinty. 'I didn't realise congratulations were in order,' he murmured thoughtfully.

'Surely my engagement had nothing to do with this?' she persisted waspishly.

'No—no, of course not.' The ingratiating smile was back. 'I'm sure we can fit the work we do together around your wedding plans. Do you have an assistant I can deal with after your marriage?'

'I intend to continue working after my marriage,' Kate told him distantly.

'You do?' He seemed surprised.

'Of course,' she nodded coolly. 'Although I wouldn't dream of letting my marriage interfere with my work for you.'

'Oh, but—Please, you—you mustn't let us delay any of your plans.' He seemed to be becoming increasingly agitated. 'I'm sure your fiancé wouldn't thank me—us, for that.'

'He understands,' she said confidently, knowing she didn't really speak the truth. She quite expected the agency to become a bone of contention between Richard and herself once they were married; it was the price she would have to pay for being the wife of a rich and influential man. It was a small price to pay for that privilege, she thought hardly.

'I'm sure he does,' again that unnatural smile creased his features. 'But it won't hurt to try and fit things in around your busy schedule this end.'

Kate frowned, not at all sure of this sudden capitulation, of his ingratiating manner; it didn't sit well on this austere man. 'Do I take that to mean I'm being considered for your new advertising contract?' Her tone was abrupt.

His smile was tight now. 'I'm sure you know you can take it to mean much more than that.'

'I can?'

'Let's not be coy, Miss Collier,' he said almost wearily. 'The contract is already yours. There was never any doubt about that.'

Her eyes began to glow, deeply gold in her pleasure. She leant forward to shake his hand, collecting up the sheets of paper that were strewn across his desk. 'I can't tell you how grateful I am,' she said with breathless excitement. 'I'm sure you won't regret giving me this chance.' She would make sure he didn't. So Richard's influence had helped her—she would make sure it was her own hard work that Colin Harkness appreciated, and not the fact that she was about to marry a rich man.

'Let's hope not,' he bit out with a bitter twist to his mouth. 'The legal department should have your contract ready by the end of the week, so I'll be in touch. I mustn't keep you, I'm sure you have more important things to do than see me.'

More important things? The man must be mad! Admitted, she hadn't liked his manner at all, had thought him a supercilious snob, had strongly objected to his method of putting her through the hoop, but as long as she got the contract at the end of it, and was able to show him the extent of her talent, then she didn't really give a damn about Colin Harkness's manner. He would soon see that she had more to offer than an influential fiancé!

'How did it go?' Beryl demanded to know when Kate got back to the office.

'We got it!' she laughed happily, seeing no reason to tell anyone *how* she had got it; it was up to her to prove she had deserved it on her own merit.

'That's marvellous! Oh, Kate——!' Beryl stopped her as she opened the door to her private office. 'There's someone inside waiting to see you,' she grimaced as Kate turned back to her.

Kate's expression instantly became guarded. 'Who?'

Her secretary seemed disconcerted. 'You remember the man who brought in the roses yesterday——'

'Too well!' her mouth tightened. 'Okay, Beryl, thanks.' Her expression was forbidding as she entered her office, closing the door behind her to lean back against it.

Jared sat behind her desk, leaning the chair back on two legs, his feet resting on the top of her desk. He removed these slowly and sat forward, all the time his gaze searching her face. 'You got it,' he finally breathed. 'You did, didn't you, Katharine Mary?' He stood up, still wearing the black cords and yellow tee-shirt, although a light bomber jacket had been casually pulled on over the latter. 'I'm proud of you——'

'How did you get in here?'

He quirked dark brows at her icy tone. 'Do I detect a note of frost in the air?'

'More than a note,' she told him tightly. 'Jared, what are you doing here?' She crossed the room to confront him across the desktop.

His head was tilted at an angle of disbelief. 'Does this mean you *didn't* get it?'

'I just want to know what you're doing here!'

'I came to celebrate with you, Katharine Mary.' He bent behind the desk to lift up an ice-bucket, a bottle of champagne nestling on a bed of ice, and placed it on the desk, bending down again to produce two glasses.

'By the way, that wasn't kind,' he reprimanded sternly as he popped the cork from the bottle, deftly managing to pour the bubbly liquid into the waiting glasses without spilling a drop.

Kate watched him with frustrated anger. 'What wasn't?'

'Those roses cost me a small fortune.' He handed her a glass full of bubbling champagne. 'And they've all been relegated to the outer office.' He looked at her in challenge.

'I'm allergic——'

He looked as sceptical as Beryl had yesterday when she had given her the same excuse, his snort of disbelief adding to the emotion. 'You weren't allergic to the rose room service sent up on our trays at the hotel,' he drawled.

Colour immediately flooded her cheeks. 'Well, I'm allergic to them en masse,' she snapped, taking a large swallow of the champagne. 'And where did you get this from?' She held up her glass accusingly. 'I thought you were too broke to pay for a hotel room last night.'

'Did I say that?'

'You know you did,' she told him heatedly.

'Well, I managed to scrape enough together to buy a cheap bottle of champagne——'

'No champagne is cheap!'

'Will you stop arguing, woman, and tell me if we're celebrating or drowning our sorrows!'

'*We* aren't doing anything.' Her eyes flashed. 'I've already told you no man is going to get a free ride through life on me again!'

Jared's mouth tightened as he drew in a deep breath. 'Bitterness isn't pretty, Kate,' he rasped.

'Too bad!' she snapped.

He gave a frustrated sigh. 'Have I ever asked you for anything?' he enquired mildly. 'Besides the use of a bed for the night?'

'Brian never used to ask either,' she said resentfully. 'I was so besotted with him I *gave* him everything I had to give.'

Jared's mouth twisted. 'And do you think there's a possibility you could become that "besotted" with me?'

'Never!' she denied heatedly.

'Then you have nothing to worry about, do you?' he taunted. 'Drink your champagne, Katharine Mary, and stop scowling.'

It was like trying to push back the tide to deflate this man—and the tide had no more intention of turning back for her than it had for King Canute—in fact, it threatened to drown her!

She sat down wearily in the chair he had recently vacated, sipping her champagne as instructed, looking up at Jared as he sat on the edge of her desk, perilously close to her. 'Why did I ever get involved with you?' she sighed.

He grinned unconcernedly. 'Just think of me as a salve to your wounded ego that went wrong.'

'You can say that again!'

'Do I need to?' he mocked.

'No,' she grimaced. 'We all have to make at least one mistake in our lives, you must be mine.'

'I may not be a mistake at all,' he dismissed lightly. 'Now tell me if you got the Melford contract—I've waited long enough for my answer. And you've already drunk my champagne!'

Her eyes sparkled with happiness as she looked up at him. 'I got it. I didn't think I would, but I actually got it!' The adrenalin flowed through her veins at the thought of the work ahead of her.

Jared pulled her to her feet, urging her into his body as he stood with his legs apart. 'I knew you would,' he smiled down at her, his eyes glowing. 'You're a very clever and talented woman, my love.'

She also had a fiancé who seemed to wield some power, but that was no one's affair but her own. 'How do you know that?' she teased.

'Because you make love to me beautifully,' he told her huskily.

She pulled away from him with an angry glare. 'Will you forget that!' she snapped. 'Just forget I was ever stupid enough to become involved with you at the hotel.'

'I'll try,' he shrugged. 'But I doubt I can really forget the two most important days in my life.'

'Just try!' She evaded the warmth of his gaze, although the champagne in the middle of the day had made her feel a little lightheaded.

He shrugged. 'Have you told Richard of your success yet?'

'Not yet——'

'Oh, good, you can take me out to lunch, then.' He looked pleased with himself.

'I'll do no such thing——'

'Why not, you have to eat, don't you?'

'But not with you!'

'Katharine Mary,' the quiet sternness of his voice rebuked her, 'who gave you the breakfast this morning that gave you the strength to go out and captivate Harkness?'

'It was *my* food——'

'But who cooked it for you?'

Clear golden eyes battled with mocking blue ones for several minutes, until finally the fight went out of her. 'Lunch,' she nodded abruptly. 'As you said, I have to eat anyway.'

'So gracious!' Jared straightened. 'Are you sure you won't mind being seen out with me?'

Colour entered her cheeks at the warranted barb. Jared hadn't had to come here this morning to help her celebrate, once again he had been thoughtful and generous. Richard had had the same knowledge of her appointment with Colin Harkness, and yet so far he had made no effort to find out its outcome.

She was doing it again! And for the second time Richard was coming out the loser. Jared was a drifter, a roamer, she had to remember that. She *had* to.

'I don't mind at all,' she told him coolly, going to the door.

'By the way,' Jared joined her, 'I think I should answer your question of earlier—your secretary let me in here because I told her I'm your brother.'

She turned to him furiously. 'You did *what*?'

'I told her——'

'I heard you! But, unlike Ben, Beryl *knows* I don't have a brother,' she groaned.

He had the grace to look uncomfortable. 'She let me come in here anyway,' he shrugged.

Kate chewed on her bottom lip. 'And I know why. Now my secretary thinks I have a lover as well as a fiancé!'

'And don't you?'

The softly spoken question stopped her in her tracks, paling slightly as she stared up at him. Yes, she was engaged to Richard, would become his wife next month, but the man at her side was her lover every time he looked at her, his eyes possessing her at a glance, every touch of his hand a caress.

'We'd better be going,' she said abruptly. 'I only give myself an hour for lunch like everyone else has.'

'Kate,' he touched her cheek gently, 'you'll have to resolve this situation some time, why not sooner than later?'

She jerked away from him, her mouth firming. 'It already is resolved as far as I'm concerned; I'm going to marry Richard. But I have no objection to buying you lunch.'

Jared seemed about to argue with her, but finally,

with a resigned shrug, he followed her out of the office, his arm going about her shoulders as he fell into step beside her. 'Mother sends her love,' he told her lightly as they passed Beryl's desk. 'And little Michael is doing very well at school. Goodbye, Mrs Lane,' he smiled charmingly at Beryl on their way out of the door. 'It was nice to have met you.'

'You too—er—Mr—Collier . . .?' she finished lamely.

Kate gave Jared a sharp dig in the ribs with her elbow before he could make a reply. 'I'll be back in an hour,' she told the other woman distantly. 'If Richard calls tell him I'll ring him back later.'

'Er—yes, of course.' Beryl was still giving Jared speculative looks as Kate and he left together.

Jared rubbed his ribs in exaggerated pain as they went down in the lift together. 'That hurt, you know,' he frowned across at her.

'Tough!'

'You're a hard woman, Katharine Mary Collier,' he winced as if his ribs really were bruised.

'Terrible, isn't it?' Kate said unconcernedly as she unlocked her car as it stood in the reserved space in the undergound car park beneath the building, then she slid in behind the wheel, watching with some amusement as Jared folded his length into the seat next to her. The low sports car was not built for someone of his proportions. 'Comfortable?' she mocked as she started the engine, his knees almost touching his chin.

'Very,' he returned dryly.

'A jab in the ribs was the least you deserved just now,' she told him in a preoccupied voice as she and a taxi vied for position in the heavy lunchtime traffic. With a feeling of resignation she slowed her car down to a position behind the black taxi—after all, it was bigger than she was. 'My mother and father live in

Gibraltar. And who on earth is little Michael supposed to be?' She gave him a brief sideways glance.

'Our baby brother,' he grinned, his ribs forgotten.

Her mouth twisted derisively. 'Beryl already knows I don't have so much as one brother, let alone two! You made an absolute idiot of yourself just now.'

He shrugged dismissively. '"To the victor go the spoils". Or something like that,' he grinned.

'Hm?' she frowned her puzzlement.

'That rock on your finger you call a ring may say you belong to another man, but *I'm* the one you drank the champagne with, *I'm* the one you've having your celebration lunch with. I'll convince you yet that there's more to life than a career and marrying a rich man.'

'I doubt it.'

'The career I don't mind,' he spoke almost as if to himself. 'I've always admired a woman who can make it in the business world. But I've never thought a person's eligibility should be gauged by how much they earn.'

'No?' she said bitterly, her manner aggressive as she parked and locked the car outside the small Italian restaurant they were to eat at, where the food was good and not too expensive, and a table always obtainable. 'Money means power,' she told him grimly. 'Over things and people. I want that power for myself, not to become a victim of it.'

'And what will it get you?'

'Freedom!' she told him with feeling. 'Freedom to do what I want, be what I want.'

They were shown to a quiet table in the corner of the restaurant. Kate was a regular customer here, and the waiter greeted her by name before taking their order.

'How can you be free married to a man you don't love?'

She looked up to find Jared staring at her across the table, the subject she had thought forgotten during the last five minutes as they gave their order still very much in his mind. 'Who says I don't love Richard?' she defended.

'I do.'

She flushed. 'You know nothing of my feelings.'

'I know that you still respond to me when I kiss you.' Jared's eyes were narrowed and watchful.

'I still respond to him too,' her mouth twisted mockingly. 'So what does that prove?'

He drew in a ragged breath. 'Is he your lover?'

Her head went back proudly at this personal question. 'Don't you know?' she scorned.

His avid gaze searched her face, the fearless gold eyes, the almost arrogantly high cheekbones, the short nose and generous curve of a mouth, the determined chin. 'Yes, I know,' he seemed to visibly relax. 'You made love with Brian because you loved him, I was a refuge from a pain you couldn't bear alone, Richard James is the man who will give you the power you crave. No, he hasn't been your lover yet, because so far in your relationship you've found no reason for him to be.'

Kate stiffened at Jared's derisive tone. 'I'm not that mercenary——'

'You used me, you're using Richard James.'

She turned away. 'I don't want to argue with you here, Jared,' she glanced about them selfconsciously.

'We'll always argue, anywhere, until you break your engagement.'

'And marry you!'

'You're getting the idea, Katharine Mary,' he nodded, his mouth curved into a triumphant smile.

'It's your idea, not mine,' she muttered, turning with a polite smile to the waiter as he arrived to serve their meal. 'Could we drop that subject while we're eating?' she requested wearily once they were alone again. 'We're supposed to be celebrating,' she reminded him.

'So we are,' he agreed lightly. 'And now that you're going to be head of a highly successful and *powerful* advertising agency perhaps you could give me some advice on finding myself a job.'

'I thought you said there was no hurry?' She looked over at him interestedly as she took a sip of her wine.

He shrugged. 'There wasn't. But now I have to prove to the woman I want to marry that I can hold down a steady job. She won't even consider me otherwise,' he mocked.

'She isn't considering you at all, job or no job! Do your thoughts all lead back to the same subject?'

Jared gave an inclination of his head, his dark hair showing red highlights from the overhead lighting. 'I'm a very single-minded person.'

'Well, let's try and get it on to the subject of a job for you. What can you do?'

'Anything.'

Kate sighed her impatience. 'Don't be difficult, Jared. What jobs have you done in the past?'

He gave the matter some thought. 'I can turn my hand to most things. Really,' he insisted as Kate looked like giving him another set-down. 'My contacts in the business world should tell you that. I've done everything, from being a general dogsbody to being assistant to the Chairman of a company.'

Her eyes widened in disbelief. Jared didn't give the impression that he had ever sat behind a desk—to work!—in his life, let alone held down such an important position.

'I know,' his mouth twisted ruefully. 'I don't exactly look the part. But I did do it. I just prefer to dress casually whenever I can.'

Kate still frowned. 'And when did you leave this job as assistant to the Chairman?'

'I didn't exactly leave . . .'

'You were sacked!' She shook her head derisively.

'Well . . . not exactly.'

'They *asked* you to leave,' she taunted. 'Really, Jared, you don't have a very good track record. Sacked from that job, walking out on the Canadian one!'

He gave a rueful shrug, 'I bore easily.'

'And yet you say you want a wife! You're impossible, Jared,' she smiled teasingly. 'You would probably go off on your wanderings after only a month of marriage!'

'I'd take you with me.'

'I have no intention of living the rest of my life out of a suitcase,' she told him with haughty disdain. 'That's why I want to get a permanent job. What do you think I should try for? What sort of job would be acceptable for you in a future husband?'

'Head of a thriving and successful business,' she derided.

'Joking apart.'

'I wasn't joking!'

'I thought not,' he sighed. 'Well, I'll have to work my way up to that. What sort of business should it be? Not food stores, that isn't nearly grand enough for you. Men's clothing would be acceptable, I'm sure,' he mocked Richard's female clothing stores. 'I don't think I could sell men's clothing all day. I know,' his expression brightened. 'I could always model the stuff, what would you think of that?'

'Have you ever modelled before?' she asked dryly.

'No . . . But it can't be that difficult, surely? Don't you think I could do it?'

She didn't doubt he had the body and charisma to do the job, or that he had the ability; he had already shown that he could do most things he set his mind to. But the thought of him being ogled by thousands of other women was somehow unpalatable to her.

'I'm sure you could,' she said coolly. 'But would you really want to be just a clothes-peg? It can be a very degrading profession. I wouldn't——' Her attention was caught and held by the voluptuous blonde woman just entering the restaurant, her riveted gaze passing quickly to the man at her side, her breath leaving her in a relieved sigh as she saw it wasn't the man she had thought to see. This man's hair was iron-grey.

Kate wasn't aware of the keen blue eyes following her stricken gaze, of Jared's eyes narrowing as he too watched the other couple being seated across the room from them. Kate had gone very pale, and the confidence he had come to associate with her seemed to be crumbling before his eyes.

'I wasn't going to be a nude model,' he lightly drew her attention back to him.

Kate blinked at him blankly for several seconds, then she mentally berated herself. There was no reason to be so disconcerted by seeing Coral Linton—after all, they all lived in London, meetings like this were sure to happen from time to time. But why this restaurant? It wasn't exactly the sort of place she would have expected Coral to patronise, surely it was too quiet for her tastes. And it was her own and Brian's restaurant! Perhaps that was what shocked her the most, not that Coral was obviously here enjoying herself with someone who wasn't her husband, but that it was probably Brian who had introduced his wife to 'their' restaurant.

As she looked at Jared her mask of sophistication was firmly back in place. 'Don't you think you would qualify?' she mocked.

'I don't know—would I?'

Her husky laugh was perfectly controlled, the woman seated across the restaurant from them ignored for the moment. 'I think you would make a very good nude model.'

Jared returned the smile with intimacy. 'I love your body too, Katharine Mary.' He held her gaze with his.

To her chagrin she was the first to look away, her gaze drifting over to where Coral was talking animatedly to her dining-companion, the man looking to be in his early to late forties, very good-looking in a world-weary sort of way. As if she had become aware of being watched sharp blue eyes were turned to meet Kate's across the room, widening with recognition. Kate looked away slowly, more disconcerted than she cared to show.

'Not hungry?'

Once again her attention returned to Jared, and she smiled her apology for not eating her meal. 'Not really.' She put down her knife and fork. 'You?' She noticed for the first time that he was no longer eating either; there was almost as much food left on his plate as her own.

'No. Would you like to leave now?'

She knew it would be running away, but she couldn't help it. Seeing Coral Linton had reminded her of all she had lost. But before they could get up to leave a shadow fell over their table, and Kate looked up to find Coral standing there.

'I hope you don't mind my coming over,' the other woman gushed, 'but I felt I just had to say hello after all this time.'

Kate didn't know why the other woman should feel such a compulsion. The last—and only time!—they had ever met, Coral had made it only too clear that she would rather not see Kate again, at any time.

And it seemed she hadn't changed her mind about that; she was smiling provocatively at Jared and ignoring Kate. 'It's been so long since I last saw you, darling,' she purred, her blue eyes seductive. 'Where have you been hiding yourself?'

Jared lounged back in his chair, his hands thrust nonchalantly into the pockets of his cords, a light of flirtation in the mocking blue eyes, his smile one of sensuality. 'Here and there, Coral,' he drawled softly. 'I hear you got married recently?'

Coral's mouth tightened, the red lips pouting. 'That's right,' her voice was brittle. 'But then we all make mistakes.'

'It doesn't sound as if it's a complete success,' he derided her bored tone.

'It's no bed of roses living with an artist.' The other woman turned taunting blue eyes on Kate. 'You know that, don't you?'

'Do I?' she returned stiffly.

'Of course.' Coral gave a throaty laugh. 'Still, the loss of Brian doesn't seem to have affected you too badly, does it? I saw the announcement of your engagement in the newspaper only this morning, and now here you are out with Jared. I'll tell Brian you're managing just fine without him, shall I?'

'If you wish,' Kate nodded distantly.

'Oh, I do.' The other woman's laugh was taut now. 'It will give me an answer to the way he sings your praises night and day.' Her eyes were as hard as ice. 'I felt sure you couldn't be the paragon he made you out to be, now I know you aren't. Still, we all have our little—indiscretions, don't we?' She looked pointedly at the man waiting for her return to their table. 'It's been really good to see you again, Jared. You must call me. You still have my number?'

He nodded, his cool confidence not having slipped for even a moment during the exchange.

But Kate's had! It was obvious that Jared and Coral had once been very close—intimate? Was it possible that Jared had once been the other woman's lover? Fate couldn't be that cruel to her!

CHAPTER FIVE

'WHAT do you want to know?' Jared drawled in answer to her question about Coral and himself.

The two of them had driven back to Kate's office in silence, shocked silence on her part. To know that Jared and Coral knew each other, on a more than friendly basis, she felt sure, had made her speechless, although she just had to know the truth about them now.

'Isn't it obvious?' she said tautly.

Jared sat on the edge of her desk, his foot resting on the chair in front of him. 'Not to me,' he shook his head, query still in the deep blue eyes.

Kate's eyes flared her anger at him. 'You realise who she is, of course?' she snapped.

'Well, of course I realise,' he mocked with humour. 'It was me she wanted to talk to, remember?'

'That much was obvious.' She moved restlessly about the room. 'But you *knew* she was the woman who had married my ex-fiancé, and yet you said nothing!'

'What could I say?' he shrugged.

'That you'd slept with the woman who's now married to Brian!'

'As I remember,' he said thoughtfully, 'there wasn't much sleeping involved in my relationship with Coral; she's a very passionate woman,' he drawled.

'So Brian told me.' Kate's hands were clasped agitatedly together in front of her, her face very pale. 'So you did have an affair with her?' She looked at Jared with pained eyes.

'Not exactly.' He watched the tip of his boot as he

swung his foot backwards and forwards. 'Coral wanted more than I was able to give, I'm afraid. She demands a man's full and absolute attention,' he went on to explain casually. 'Something I wasn't prepared—or able—to give her at the time.'

'And now?' Kate bit out tautly.

'Now she's a married lady,' he shrugged dismissal of the subject, his eyes a clear untroubled blue as he met her gaze.

Kate's mouth was taut. 'That doesn't seem to inhibit her in the least! You realise that the man with her just now wasn't Brian?'

His mouth twisted. 'I had an idea—unless you're into much older men. And I don't think you are.'

'No,' she acknowledged tightly. 'And I don't think the fact that she wears a wedding ring is going to stop her having an affair with you.'

'It stops me.'

'Why?' she scorned. 'I wear a ring and yet you seem determined to have me.'

'Marry you,' Jared corrected gravely. 'And you only wear an engagement ring, that still makes you a free agent in my book—unless of course it was my ring you were wearing,' he added mockingly. 'Then it would be a different matter altogether.'

'That isn't even a possibility!' Especially now. To know that Jared too had fallen victim to the other woman's charms in the past filled Kate with dismay.

Jared seemed to read her thoughts easily, for he stood up to take her in his arms, quietening her struggles to be free with ease. 'The past is the past, Katharine Mary,' he told her softly. 'It can never be undone. I haven't condemned you for the fact that you went to bed with Brian before we met.'

'I went to bed with him because I loved him!' She glared up at him.

'I'm well aware of that. I'm also well aware that I

felt no such emotion for Coral, or she for me. We desired each other. I think we met twice, maybe three times,' he dismissed. 'That doesn't even amount to an affair. Besides, I don't remember you complaining at the hotel about the experience I'd acquired with women like Coral,' he taunted.

Hot colour flooded her cheeks, as she remembered vividly the way he had been able to fire her to burning passion within seconds, knowing all the pleasure spots, seeking out all the erotic areas of her body with remorseless hands and mouth. In his arms she hadn't just seen the earth move, she had seen it swing on its axis! Experience for experience, Jared gave her more passion and pleasure than Brian ever had. But there was more to making love than being able to perform the act well, there was love and all its inherent emotions. And love had never entered her sexual encounter with Jared. Even though he spoke of marriage now he hadn't mentioned the word love to her.

And if he had, would she still be so determined not to become involved with him? Of course she would. Jared was *not* the man for her!

And yet even now she couldn't pull away from him, she felt mesmerised by the warmth in deep blue eyes, the hard strength in the body that fitted so perfectly against hers. 'Jared . . .!' she hardly recognised that heartfelt groan as coming from her own throat, that tortuous longing was surely not within her.

'I know, darling,' he soothed, his hands curved possessively about her hips, holding her into him, feeling her tremble at the aroused hardness of his body. 'I want you too, but I've made myself a promise, one I intend keeping.'

'You have?' She arched her throat into him as his lips travelled over her silky skin.

'Yes,' he groaned, then his mouth claimed hers, parting her lips to probe the deep warmth within.

'And what promise is that?' she breathed against his lips as he at last raised his head.

'Not to make love to you again until that ring is off your finger and the promise to marry me is in its place.' One of his hands moved to cup her breast.

For a few brief seconds his words didn't sink in, lost as she was in the euphoria of his caressing fingertips. And then his words struck home, and she looked up at him with dazed golden eyes. 'What did you say?' she gasped.

His expression was hard, his mouth firm. 'I don't intend being any woman's bit of forbidden sex, the man she goes to when she has a free afternoon from the hairdressers and her husband is out at work so that he can keep her in the luxury to which she's decided she wants to become accustomed.'

Kate pulled completely out of his arms, staring up at him with wide disbelieving eyes. 'Is that really what you think of me?'

'Why else would you marry Richard James?' he shrugged. 'You certainly don't love him.'

'I respect him,' she defended.

Jared's eyes became flinty. 'And you don't respect me?'

It was crazy to feel actual pain by what he was saying to her, and yet she did, feeling a need to hurt him in return. 'How can I possibly respect a man who says he lives on his wits, which is just another way of saying he moves from one woman to the next, living off them until the next one comes along?' she scorned contemptuously.

Jared was very pale, his eyes icing over. 'That's what you think, is it?' he rasped.

'Coral seems to make a habit of helping "needy" young men who will be dependent on her.' Her mouth twisted derisively. 'And you can't deny that you've been sleeping and eating at my flat the last two days, free of charge.'

'So I'm no better than a gigolo, am I?'

'No, I didn't mean——'

'Didn't you?' he taunted coldly. 'I happen to think you did. Maybe I've been wrong about you after all, Kate. You choose to know people only as you see them—either you can't, or don't want to see beneath the surface. Brian Linton seems to be the man you really want,' he bit out contemptuously. 'And from what Coral was saying about their marriage earlier he may soon be free to come back to you.' His gaze raked over her with open disgust. 'I'm sorry I ever met you!'

'Jared——' The door slammed behind him as he left.

Damn him! Why did he have to keep intruding into her life, making outrageous statements before leaving again? *Could* it possibly be true that Brian's marriage was already floundering? Coral had seemed to imply that it was, she had also seemed to be saying it was partly Kate's fault. But she wouldn't want Brian now if he were to come back to her, would she? No, of course not. He had shown his true nature when he had let her down so badly with Coral.

As she had shown hers when she threw those hateful accusations at Jared just now? What was it about him that made her do and say such things! Of course she didn't believe he was a gigolo, he had never asked her for anything, and Coral had been the one doing the chasing today, not the other way around.

Could that really be the root of the trouble, was she jealous of his past relationship with the other woman? To feel jealousy she would have to admit to being in love with him—and not even to herself was she prepared to make such an admission about Jared.

She wrenched open her office door. 'Beryl!' she

rasped, ignoring the other woman's surprised expression at her aggression. 'If my "brother" ever comes here again I do not want to see him. Is that understood?' she grated.

'Yes, but——'

'Good,' she bit out abruptly. 'Did Richard call?' she rasped.

'No.'

'Oh.' Kate's mouth tightened, her humour not improved at all by this information. 'Could you get him on the line for me? Now,' she added curtly as Beryl made no effort to do so.

'Oh—oh, of course.' Her secretary at once began to make the call.

Kate went back into her office, closing the door to lean back against it weakly, the angry fog beginning to clear from her brain. But before it could clear completely the telephone on her desk began to ring. With a deep sigh she picked up the receiver, her hand shaking slightly as she did so. Jared made her feel such extremes of emotions, weak with desire, mindless with anger.

'Your call to Richard, Kate,' Beryl informed her distantly.

Damn, now she had upset one of her closest friends too! She would have to try and explain the reason for her temper later. Well, not exactly explain it, but——

'Kate? Kate, are you there? Is there anything wrong?'

Richard's concerned voice finally penetrated the vehement intensity of her thoughts, and she felt her anger returning as it did. 'No, nothing is wrong,' she snapped. 'Everything is right. But you didn't even bother to telephone and find out, did you? I suppose my career must seem very unimportant to you, but I——'

'Kate!' he firmly interrupted her tirade. 'What's all this about?'

'What's——! Don't you remember what today is?'

'Today? But—Oh, your meeting with Colin Harkness?' he suddenly realised. 'How did it go?'

'Do you care?'

'Well, of course I care,' he sighed his exasperation with her childishness. 'Look, I realise you're upset, Kate,' his voice gentled, 'but you really can't win them all. And I did warn you——'

'I got it,' she put in tersely, surprised that he didn't realise the power he wielded. Just the fact that she was his fiancée had been enough to make Colin Harkness knuckle under.

'—that you—What did you say?' Richard suddenly seemed to realise she had spoken.

'I got it, Richard—the Melford contract,' she revealed tightly. 'I go in and sign it at the end of the week.'

For a moment he seemed stunned, then, 'Why, that's wonderful, Kate,' he enthused. 'You clever girl! Where would you like to go to celebrate tonight?'

His reaction now was everything she could have wished for, and yet at that moment she was remembering a different sort of reaction, a quietly confident reaction that had been warming as well as encouraging. Jared had been so sure of her capabilities that he had waited here for her return with a bottle of champagne, and a short time ago she had levelled accusations at him that now made her blush with shame.

'Kate?' Richard prompted impatiently at her silence.

God, she had sent Jared away from here believing she despised him, and she didn't, she—She what? Loved him? No, she didn't love him, but she had had no right to be condescending about his way of life. So he enjoyed a life with no responsibilities or commitment, it was his life, damn it! But if he didn't want responsibility or commitment why had he asked her to marry him?

'Kate!' Richard was becoming impatient now. 'Look, there's no need to sulk just because I was a little remiss about your appointment at Melfords. I didn't——'

'I'm not sulking,' she hastily assured him. 'I never sulk,' she added lightly. 'But there's no need for us to celebrate anything.' She had already done enough of that today, with disastrous results. 'The time to celebrate will be when I make a success of it. I have months of hard work ahead of me before I can lay claim to that,' and none of Richard's wealth or influence could help her with that!

'We can still do a little quiet celebrating,' Richard suggested huskily. 'At my place?'

'That sounds nice,' she accepted softly, her burning anger of a few minutes ago having faded and died completely. 'I'll come over about eight, shall I?'

'Ever the independent woman!' he teased. 'Eight o'clock will be fine.'

Kate stared silently off into space once Richard had rung off. What would he think if he knew that once, for two very brief days, she hadn't been independent at all, that she had given herself into a man's keeping for that time, that she had felt cherished and cared for, the outside world not mattering to her at all, not even Brian?

Jared had made her feel all that, had *given* her all that, and now he was gone—and she didn't even have a telephone number where she could reach him and apologise. She might never see him again.

Richard's flat was a typical bachelor home, any feminine touches being supplied by the housekeeper who came in every day, conveniently returning to her own home in the evenings. Tonight had been no exception to that. Kate and Richard were alone as soon as dinner had been cleared away, relaxing together in the cream and black lounge.

With the eye of a trained artist, dealing with colour and settings every day, Kate could see several changes in the décor she would like to make here, ways of adding warmth, of giving character to the rooms that although stylish were sadly lacking in personality.

'So how is the work going on my new advertising campaign?' Richard came to sit beside her on the sofa after pouring each of them a glass of brandy.

'I've given it to Clarissa,' she grimaced. 'Mr Harkness has insisted that I have to do the work for Melfords myself.' She had received a call from him this afternoon instructing her to do just that, the softening in his manner she had sensed this morning completely gone.

'So you aren't going to have time to deal with my work,' Richard added dryly.

'No,' she admitted ruefully.

'I realise Melfords is important to you, Kate,' he swirled the brandy about in his bulbous glass, 'but don't forget the smaller men are the ones who have kept you in work up until now. I've put a lot of colleagues on to your agency, I would hate to think you were going to let me down.'

'Let *you* down——!'

'Now don't lose your temper, Kate,' he soothed, grasping her hand in his. 'I don't know what's got into you this last week, but you've been positively volatile. Is it because of the situation between the two of us?' he prompted softly.

'Situation between us?' Kate frowned her puzzlement. 'I don't know what you mean. We're engaged to be married——'

'And we're both adults, with adult needs,' Richard finished pointedly, his dark brows quirked above

Introducing

Harlequin Temptation™

Have you ever thought
you were in love
with one man...only
to feel attracted to another?

That's just one of the temptations you'll find facing the women in new *Harlequin Temptation* romance novels.

Sensuous...contemporary...compelling...reflecting today's love relationships!

The passionate torment of a woman torn between two loves...the siren call of a career...the magnetic advances of an impetuous employer—nothing is left unexplored in this romantic new series from Harlequin. You'll thrill to a candid new frankness as men and women seek to form lasting relationships in the face of temptations that threaten true love. Begin with your FREE copy of *First Impressions*. Mail the reply card today!

First Impressions
by Maris Soule

He was involved with her best friend.

Tracy Dexter couldn't deny her attraction to her new boss. Mark Prescott looked more like a jet set playboy than a high school principal—and he acted like one, too. It wasn't right for Tracy to go out with him, not when her friend Rose had already staked a claim. It wasn't right, even though Mark's eyes were so persuasive, his kiss so probing and intense. Even though his hands scorched her body with a teasing, raging fire...and when he gently lowered her to the floor she couldn't find the words to say no.

A word of warning to our regular readers: While Harlequin books are always in good taste, you'll find more sensuous writing in new *Harlequin Temptation* than in other Harlequin romance series.

® ™ Trademarks of Harlequin Enterprises Ltd.

Get this romance novel FREE
as your introduction to new

Harlequin Temptation ™

◁ See exciting details inside.

Canada Post
Postes Canada
708

Kate didn't hold out much hope of that ever happening, she had heard the same promise too many times since Gill had first borrowed the dishes. Oh well, she had tried.

To say she was bad-tempered the next day would be putting it mildly—she hardly knew herself.

She had slept very badly, had half expected, despite the lateness of the hour, that Jared would still put in an appearance. He hadn't. And her night's sleep had suffered because of it.

'Is there anything wrong, Kate?' Beryl came into her office towards late afternoon.

'Wrong?' Kate looked up vaguely. 'Of course there's nothing wrong, why should there be?' she scowled.

'Well, Joyce was almost in tears just now when she left your office——'

'So she should be,' Kate snapped. 'Those formats for Denison should have been halfway finished by now. I don't pay her to sit around and flirt with Bernard!'

'No, I realise that,' Beryl agreed lightly. 'I just wondered if there was anything you—you would like to talk about?'

'I don't think so,' Kate shook her head firmly.

'Only Richard has called three times today and each time you've told me to tell him you aren't in.'

'Yes?' Her eyes were narrowed.

'Well, each time you have been here.' Her secretary looked worried by her unusual behaviour. 'I just wondered if your—tension has anything to do with the brother you suddenly acquired at the beginning of the week. I know I wouldn't mind a brother like that!' she added appreciatively.

'Beryl . . .!'

'Yes?' The other woman looked at her with mischievous eyes.

Kate's anger left her with a sigh as she sat back in her chair, her hair in its usual severe style, her face pale, her eyes like liquid gold, the severity of the black and white dress she wore adding to her paleness. 'Is it that obvious?' she asked wearily.

'I don't quite know what you mean by "that".' Beryl sat on the edge of her desk. 'But I would say it's very obvious that something is bothering you. You don't exactly have the look of a newly engaged lady.'

Kate closed her eyes, rubbing her aching temples. 'If only he hadn't come back,' she muttered almost to herself. 'If only he'd stayed in America!'

'Your brother?' Beryl prompted softly.

She looked at her secretary with a tired sigh. 'Jared Rourke. I don't suppose there's been any calls from *him* today?'

Beryl pursed her lips, shaking her head. 'Not one. So his name is Jared,' she said thoughtfully. 'He certainly is a charmer.'

'Yes,' she acknowledged ruefully. 'Why is it that all the poor ones are?' she sighed.

The other woman looked puzzled. 'Would it be too much to ask where he fits into the picture?'

'He doesn't,' Kate told her flatly. 'At least, he shouldn't.'

'But he does?'

'I don't know, Beryl,' she sighed. 'I really don't know. I thought he didn't, but now he seems to have disappeared.'

'And you're worried about him?'

'Not exactly.' She leant her chin on her cupped hands, her elbows resting on the desktop in support. 'He's a grown man, he knows how to take care of himself. It's just—I wasn't very nice to him before he left yesterday, and I said some things I wish I hadn't.'

'That was when he stormed out of here?'

'Mm,' she nodded, still looking miserable.

'I shouldn't worry about it.' Beryl stood up. 'He's probably just gone off to sulk.'

Kate's mouth curved into an unwilling smile. 'Do you really think so?'

'Of course,' the other woman dismissed. 'All men are boys at heart,' she assured Kate before leaving.

Kate wished she could be as sure. She had said some pretty awful things to Jarerd yesterday, things he might not forgive her for.

The insistent ringing of her telephone had her reaching for the receiver, her response vague, to say the least.

'It's Richard again,' Beryl told her questioningly.

She would have to talk to him; she had the feeling that if she didn't he was going to be demanding some serious explanations from her.

'Kate?' he queried abruptly as he realised that he had at last been put through to her. 'A bit elusive today, aren't you?'

She deserved the rebuke, and colour darkened her cheeks at his sarcasm. 'I'm sorry, darling. I've been so busy——'

'It doesn't matter now, as long as I've finally got to speak to you.' There was still displeasure in his voice, the word finally emphasised slightly. 'About tonight——'

'Dinner at my flat,' she suggested quickly. 'I could cook your favourite Boeuf Stroganoff. And then afterwards——'

'It sounds delightful, Kate,' he cut in abruptly. 'But the reason I've been trying all day to reach you was that I have to leave town for a couple of days later this evening.'

'I—But—Why?' she frowned; he had made no mention of this before.

'Business,' came his curt reply. 'I'm having trouble with some of my designers in France. The personal touch should soon put that right,' he added with satisfaction.

'Well, if you have to go,' she bit back her disappointment. 'I shall miss you,' she told him huskily.

'I find that very difficult to believe,' Richard returned with haughty arrogance.

He was still angry with her about last night! 'Richard, I'm sorry about——'

'I don't have time to listen to apologies, Kate, especially ones that can't really mean a lot. What I will say is that perhaps we've been a little hasty in our decision to get married, that we should both give it a little more thought.'

'Oh, but——'

'I suggest you use these few days while I'm away to decide if you're really the sort of wife I want—and need,' he continued coldly. 'We'll talk when I get back.' He hung up.

Kate swallowed hard, knowing that his 'suggestion' had really been a threat, that she either did things his way or not at all. She had never known Richard to act like this before, and she felt shaken by the change that had come over him. But she had wanted to marry a powerful man, a man who could control his own life and those about him, never thinking that she would be one of them. She felt uneasy, as if she had got herself in too deeply with something that was potentially dangerous.

Two days at the most she had to decide if this was really what she wanted, and after that Richard would demand anything of her he wanted. And after last night she knew what he wanted; she realised he had just been biding his time before asking for a physical commitment from her. It was a physical commitment she didn't know if she could fulfil.

Oh, her head ached! The work for Melfords spread

out on her desk was impossible for her to do when she felt so lousy; she would be better leaving it until tomorrow. It was after four now, why shouldn't she give herself an early night for a change? She was certainly doing no good sitting here trying to sort out the mess of her life. It was thinking about that that had given her the headache in the first place!

Beryl looked up from her own work as she sensed Kate standing in front of her desk, her eyes widening as she saw she was ready to leave for the night. 'Had enough?' she queried lightly.

'I'm going to do everyone a favour and go home,' she said dryly.

'If there are any calls for you—important ones,' Beryl added pointedly, 'shall I let you know?'

By 'important' Kate knew the other woman meant from Jared, and for a brief moment she wished she hadn't been quite so candid with her friend. But where the hell was he—could he really have left her life so abruptly? What had she said yesterday that was so different from all the other insults she had levelled at him? That she didn't respect him, that he was no better than a gigolo! Heavens, had she really said those things to the man she—she what? Had spent two reckless days and nights with! It was a vicious circle, the same thoughts going round and round in her head, till she was unsure what she felt for anyone any more.

'Yes, please,' she told Beryl wearily. 'Although I very much doubt there'll be any.' The last was added with dull acceptance.

Her flat seemed even emptier and more lonely than last night, and Ben's questions about her 'brother' on the way up here had met with curt replies. Jared had truly invaded every aspect of her life, and she didn't know how she was going to survive without his unexpected visits.

Of course she would survive, she always had, hadn't

she! And once Richard was her husband she would never look back, would never again have reason to doubt that a man's interest was truly in her and not in just what she could give him financially.

Then why did her tears mingle with the shower-water as she stood beneath the refreshing spray? She hadn't cried since Brian had let her down with such disastrous results, and she had no idea why she was crying now.

Except that she suddenly felt so alone, as if her best friend had just deserted her. Which was ridiculous, considering she had never had a best friend! As a child she had moved about a lot with her parents. Her father had been in the Army then, although he was retired now, and the constant moves hadn't given her the opportunity to make lifelong friends, only fleeting ones. At college she had met and fallen in love with Brian almost immediately, and after that he had become the centre of her existence, her only companion once her parents had moved to Gibraltar to live three years ago.

Now not knowing where Jared was had reduced her to tears once again, or could it be because of Richard's almost ultimatum? She didn't know any more, she hadn't felt this confused about her emotions since she had been a mixed-up teenager, having known from the moment she met Brian when she was nineteen that they would get married and be happy together. Now he was married to someone else, and she—she was engaged to one man and yet still dangerously attracted to another one.

She was drying her hair in her bedroom mirror when the doorbell rang shortly after five. Her eyes were beginning to glow as she put the dryer down to go and answer the door. It had to be Jared this time, and just for worrying her she would make him cook the dinner tonight.

'I knew you wouldn't——' Once again she was wrong about the identity of her visitor. 'Brian . . .!' she said dazedly, staring up at him with unblinking eyes.

CHAPTER SIX

HER first thought was that he looked older. Her second that he looked very unhappy.

And that knowledge gave her none of the exhilaration she had thought she would feel if the misery he had inflicted on her when he broke their engagement so callously rebounded on him.

'Can I come in?' His voice was gruff.

Kate opened the door wider for him to enter, not saying a word, taking the few minutes it took him to walk into the lounge to collect her own thoughts together. Brian had changed considerably in the three months since she had last seen him. Beside the obvious physical changes, the weary look about his eyes, the petulant droop to his mouth, he was also slimmer, the tailored cream suit and black silk shirt he had on much more expensive than the clothes he used to wear.

The obvious elegance of his clothing made her very selfconscious of her own attire, the black silk robe over her nakedness, her hair still damp down her back, her face bare of make-up. But what did it matter how she looked? Brian was as far removed from her now as the moon was; the plain gold wedding ring on his finger, and the diamond one on her own, dictated that it had to be so.

He looked at her with velvet brown eyes, the same velvet brown eyes that had always sent a thrill of anticipation down her spine. Now she felt nothing, only curiosity as to his reason for coming here.

'I wasn't sure you would be at home yet.' His voice was still husky, a little uncertain.

She shrugged dismissively. 'I left early.'

His dark brows quirked, the same coal-black colour as the hair that was styled so neatly over his collar and ears, the same dark hair that he had assured her time and time again he didn't have the time to get cut when she had teased him about the fact that it was too long. He seemed to have found the time now. To look at him now was like looking at a stranger, a very expensively dressed, perfectly groomed stranger.

'That's unusual for you, isn't it?' he said softly, his hands thrust into his trouser pockets, as if he weren't quite sure what to do with them.

'Perhaps,' she conceded distantly.

He nodded, chewing on his inner lip. 'Er—Coral said she saw you yesterday.'

'She did,' Kate nodded.

'She was lunching with a—a friend,' the explanation seemed forced out of him. 'Paul Lincoln, actually, the man who's showing my exhibition for me.'

'Oh yes,' she nodded coolly, and moved to sit in one of the armchairs, holding her robe over her legs as she crossed one knee over the other. 'How is it going?'

A nerve began to pulsate in his jawline, his mouth tightening. 'Very well. In fact, it's a sell-out,' he revealed tautly.

He didn't look exactly pleased by the fact. 'That's good, isn't it?' Kate frowned at his attitude.

'Is it?' he said bitterly. 'A lot of high-class snobs who want "something" to hang on their wall that won't clash with the décor or furnishings!' His mouth twisted in disgust. 'That isn't what I worked myself ragged for!'

'As long as it sells . . .' she shrugged.

'That's what Coral says,' he scowled.

Kate didn't even flinch at this second mention of his wife's name, although she couldn't help wondering how much of a 'friend' Paul Lincoln was to her—he had certainly seemed more than that yesterday. She also remembered her own jealous reaction to Jared knowing the other woman.

Her eyes became hard. 'Well, it's true, isn't it?' she dismissed coldly.

'True!' Brian's expression became aggressive. 'A lot of idiots just looking for another piece of furniture! And the critics ripped me to shreds,' he groaned.

'What do they know?' she scorned. 'You always said that if the critics panned you then the exhibition was guaranteed to be a success,' she reminded him.

'Not these critics.' He looked bleak. 'Every one put the knife in.' He sank down into the chair opposite her, his face buried in his hands. 'I should never have let Coral persuade me to show in Lincoln's gallery,' he muttered, looking up at her with hard brown eyes. 'He's her lover, you know. At least, he was. He probably still is for all I know.' He scowled once again, not really looking at Kate now, his thoughts inwards.

She could see that the fact that a woman might be cheating on him was a new experience for Brian—one that he didn't like at all. 'Brian——' she began.

'I hear you got yourself engaged to some rich man in the City.' It was almost an accusation.

Kate bristled with indignation. 'That's right,' she snapped, wondering how he had the nerve to come here and complain for ten minutes about the *success* of his exhibition, and then rebuke her for trying to put her life back together after he had so callously walked out on her. 'The wedding is next month,' she added antagonistically.

'Do you love him?'

'Really, Brian,' her tone was brittle as she stood up to move about the room, 'I don't think my feelings for Richard are any of your business!'

'Coral said you were with someone else yesterday.'

'So?'

'So who was he?'

Once again she felt indignant, her eyes widening, her breath catching in her throat. 'Yet another of your wife's ex-lovers,' she snapped angrily.

For a moment he looked stunned, although he recovered quickly. 'What was his name?' His voice was deceptively soft.

'Why don't you ask her?' Kate scorned.

'I intend to,' he bit out grimly. 'God, Kate, why are we arguing?' he groaned, his eyes gently pleading. 'I didn't come here to talk about Coral, or your fiancé, or even my damn exhibition.'

She eyed him warily. 'Then what did you come here to talk about?'

'Us.'

'Us?' She moistened her lips nervously, watching him with suspicion. 'There is no us to talk about, Brian,' she reminded him. 'I've already told you that once, three months ago when you asked me to be your mistress.'

He stood up, his expression anguished. 'God, Kate, I made a mistake!' he groaned. 'I should never have given you up and married Coral.'

'As I remember it, you didn't want to give me up,' she reminded him again, derisively.

'I should have realised then that I was making a mistake,' he muttered, running a hand through the thickness of his hair, the style such that it simply fell back into place, professionally cut to look windswept. 'How could I ever have imagined I loved Coral when the thought of losing you nearly broke me up?'

She remained hardened against the ragged edge to his voice, remembering well the pain he had inflicted on her the last time she had allowed herself to feel love for him. 'No one forced you to marry her,' she said sharply.

'No,' he sighed. 'At the time I thought I was doing

the right thing. But I'm not cut out to be some sort of exhibit myself! Ever since we've been married Coral had been dragging me off to one party or another, introducing me as her artist husband as if I'm some sort of freak. And if I refuse to go there's hell to pay! Now she's come up with the idea that I should do a European tour,' he growled.

'Well?' Kate couldn't see anything wrong with that.

'I'm all burnt out from this last one,' he shook his head. 'It would take me months of intensive work to even think about giving another exhibition, either here or in Europe. And you know how I hate to be pressurised, how I like to take time over my work, feel it, enjoy it.'

Yes, she knew that. She also remembered sitting in his studio night after night in total silence as he worked, going to parties on her own because he was so engrossed in his latest 'masterpiece' he didn't have the time to go, being available and eager when he was in the mood for making love. She remembered all that, but it was no longer her concern. He was Coral's husband now.

'You always understood me, Kate.' He was standing very close to her now. 'Always knew when I needed you.' His voice had lowered, become seductive, encouraging. 'I've been a fool, Kate. Forgive me.' His hands framed her face as he bent his head to kiss her.

She was too stunned at first to do more than accept the kiss in quiet stillness, to even respond a little as she realised this was Brian kissing her, the man she had thought never to be close to again.

And then her sense of indignity reasserted itself. How *dared* he come here and kiss her? What did he think gave him the right to do this to her again? He had made his decision, his choice, he had no right to come here now and try to mess up her life a second time.

'What do you think you're doing?' She pulled away from him, pushing against his chest. 'Brian, let me go!'

'I can't,' he rained kisses over her face and down her throat, 'and you don't really want me to. Oh, Kate, it's been so awful without you. I've missed you so. Darling . . .!'

'No, Brian! No——!' She cringed away from him, trying desperately to avoid his questing lips. 'Stop it,' she cried. 'For God's sake stop it!'

His arms were like steel bands, holding her to him, refusing to release her. 'I want you so much, Kate. I *need* you. Remember how it used to be, Kate?' He looked down at her with fevered eyes. 'Remember how good it used to be, the fun we had together? It could be like that again. I made a mistake, but we don't both have to pay for it for the rest of our lives.'

'Brian, stop this . . .' She was beginning to feel faint, overpowered by the fierceness of his kisses, the strength of his arms that wouldn't relinquish her, crushing her against him.

'You don't really mean that,' he told her confidently. 'I'll divorce Coral and marry you. It can all be as it used to be, just the two of us. You have the agency, and I can concentrate on getting ready for a new exhibition.' Enthusiasm fired his voice, his face glowing. 'I could move in here straight away, and we could turn the spare bedroom into a studio——'

'Brian!'

At last her lack of enthusiasm for the plans he was so feveredly making seemed to get through to him. 'You don't like that idea, hmm?' he frowned thoughtfully. 'Well, I suppose I could always arrange to rent a studio. The security on that could be a little hard to organise, but I——'

'Brian. I don't think I'm getting through to you!' Kate was breathing hard in her vehemence. 'There isn't going to be a studio here or anywhere else as far as I'm concerned,' she glared at him with fury. 'Because you aren't coming here either. Have I made myself clear enough?' she demanded angrily.

He slowly released her, looking down at her with dazed eyes. 'What do you mean?'

'You mean you don't know?' she said with bitter sarcasm.

Lord, this man must think she was a complete idiot where he was concerned! She had to admit that for a moment she had been tempted to respond to his kisses, to give in to the impulse and to hell with his marriage to Coral. But that impulse had only been fleeting, knowing that what she was doing was wrong.

And thank God she had. What Brian was proposing was to use her once again, to let her be his meal ticket, knowing she would never be as forceful or pushy as Coral appeared to have been. Perhaps *she* hadn't been that way once, but that had all changed in the last three months, the blinkers of a blind, mindless love had at last lifted to show her the true man. Brian was everything that was shallow in a man; he simply used people and gave nothing in return. She had known that three months ago, all he had done was confirm it. He had also shown her that in marrying Richard she was acting as shallowly as he, that to marry him without loving him would be unfair to them both.

'Kate . . .?' He still looked puzzled about her attitude to what he had thought was a good plan.

'I'll say it a little more plainly for you, Brian,' she told him between gritted teeth. 'Just so that there'll be no more misunderstandings, no more visits like this one. Three months ago you made a decision to break our engagement and marry Coral, as far as I'm concerned you're stuck with it!'

'Darling . . .!'

How could he manage to sound so reproachful, so hurt! His conceit was truly incredible.

'Let me show you how good it always was between us——'

'Keep away from me!' She backed off, her face twisted with contempt as he tried once again to take her into his arms. 'I can't believe you, Brian, I really can't,' she shook her head. 'I thought I knew you. I really thought I finally did, but I didn't think even you could go this far. Two months ago you married the woman you're supposed to love—doesn't that mean anything to you?' She looked at him with incredulous eyes.

'It means I made a mistake——'

'And you made an even bigger one when you decided to come here tonight,' she told him vehemently. 'I don't want you back, Brian,' she scorned. 'In fact, I don't know what I ever saw in you in the first place!'

He looked stunned. 'You can't really mean that——'

'Every word,' Kate snapped, losing her patience completely. 'There's more I would like to say, but I'm too much of a lady to use such language. I'd like you to leave now,' she added woodenly.

'But, darling——'

Her eyes were like gold—and just as hard, cutting off any further pleading on his part. 'I believe you know the way out.'

'But you—you love me!' He sounded astounded now.

Her mouth twisted, with derision, for herself. 'No, I don't, Brian. I'm wondering now if I ever did.' She was also wondering how she could have let a man like this influence the decisions she had made about her future life, how bitterness over losing *him* could make her enter into an engagement that meant nothing to her; she wasn't even missing Richard; she knew she never would. 'You have your rich and influential wife,

Brian, I'd advise you to go back to her, before she decides she made a mistake too.'

He was breathing heavily, his eyes glittering venomously. 'Damn you!' he rasped raggedly.

'And *thank* you,' she told him quietly, 'for saving me from the greatest unhappiness of my life.' She knew now that even if she had married Brian he would still have betrayed her one day. He was that sort of man, always wanting what was just out of his grasp. He and Coral seemed to deserve each other.

'You've become hard, Kate,' he muttered as she moved to open the door for him to leave.

She nodded. 'Perhaps. But it beats living in your world of makebelieve. Try and make a success of your marriage, Brian,' she added in a softer voice. 'I'm sure you could make it work if you wanted it to.'

'Maybe I don't want to,' he growled aggressively on his way out of the door.

Kate quickly closed it after him, her breath leaving her in a relieved sigh; it could have turned out so much nastier than it had. Although she doubted Brian would ever 'sing her praises night and day' to Coral again!

And she—she had left that world of bitterness that had made her cold and calculating these last months. She looked down at the diamond ring on her finger, knowing she had no right to wear it. As soon as Richard returned she would tell him she couldn't marry him and give him the ring back. The accusations Jared had levelled at her about her engagement were all true, but she had finally come to her senses. Was it too late? Had Jared gone for good? They could have had something special together, she knew that now. She might even one day have decided she wouldn't mind living out of a suitcase with him!

The door behind her was suddenly kicked open with such violence that the force of it sent her crashing forward to sprawl on the floor. Her panicked gaze took in the lividly angry face, the usually laughing blue eyes like ice now, the sensual mouth a twist of vicious fury, the body beneath the faded denims and matching shirt tensed as if ready to spring at any moment.

Kate flinched as with two long strides Jared was inside her flat, the door seeming to rattle on its hinges as he slammed it behind him. She clutched at the lapels of her robe as he came to stand over her, unable to do anything about the bareness of her legs, the material somehow caught up beneath her. And she daren't move; Jared's anger was truly ominous.

His mouth twisted as he saw the fear in her eyes. 'You're right to be frightened of me,' he bit out grimly. 'When I lose my temper anything can happen!'

The warning was unnecessary, the clenched fists at his sides telling her well enough of the violence in him, a violence that could so easily be allowed its freedom. She daren't move, daren't speak; she just stared up at him with mute fear.

'It's only ever happened twice before,' he continued in a dangerously soft voice. 'The first time I broke my hand punching in another man's jaw, the second time I crashed my car into a tree to stop myself from killing someone. Only tonight there's no man to punch, and no tree to crash into.' His eyes began to glow like sapphires. 'There's only you,' he growled.

Kate swallowed hard, moistening her suddenly dry lips, looking up at him with stricken eyes. 'What's wrong, Jared?' she pleaded weakly. 'What's happened?'

' "What's wrong, Jared? What's happened" ' he cruelly mimicked the fear that shook her voice. 'You really need to ask that?'

She swallowed again, not recognising the man usually filled with laughter in this coldly angry stranger. 'Yes,' she quivered, knowing by the fresh flare of anger in his eyes that just that one word had been the wrong thing to say. She began to tremble.

'Much as it pleases me to have you at my feet,' he ground out fiercely, 'I'd much rather have you face me while I tell you what I think of you!' He bent to grasp her arms with strong fingers, pulling her roughly to her feet, the indentation of his fingers biting into her arms as he began to shake her. 'The first time I saw you I told myself you were different from any other woman I'd ever known. Different!' he derided his own belief of her. 'I had no idea just *how* different you are. You used me to salve your ego,' he accused with contempt. 'God, it could have been any one of the men staying in the hotel that you chose——'

'No!'

'Yes,' he hissed. 'Only it meant more to me than that, a lot more. At least, it did.'

'D-did?' Kate still trembled.

'Yes—did. When we met again I told myself you'd been hurt, that you'd realise the mistake you were making before any marriage to Richard James could take place. Only you haven't been making a mistake, have you, Kate, neither you or Linton? It all fell into place just now when I saw him leave your flat. Neither of you loses anything by marrying other people, you'll still be able to keep each other, and you'll get all that lovely money too. I was so wrong about you—I wasn't to be your lover once you were married to James, Linton was!'

She shook her head. 'No——'

'Do you deny he was here just now?' His eyes glittered down at her. 'Or that you've been thoroughly kissed?'

'No . . .' She suddenly felt sick, her stomach doing somersaults. 'Jared, please, it wasn't that way! I had no idea Brian was going to come here——'

'No?' He looked sceptical.

'No!'

'I don't believe you,' he snarled. 'But then that isn't surprising, is it?' he scorned. 'You've had me labelled for a fool since we first met.'

'Jared, that isn't true,' she cried pleadingly. 'It isn't true!'

'Oh yes, it's true,' he said savagely. 'When did you and Linton get back together, before or after his wedding to Coral? How did he persuade you to forgive him for marrying her in the first place? Do you love him so much you just *don't care*?'

'We aren't back together——'

'Liar!' Jared shouted. 'I know the way you look when you've been made love to, Kate, and you have that look now.' His gaze moved insultingly over her body. 'Do you have anything on under that robe?' he taunted, strong hands pulling the material apart, her body bared to his contemptuous gaze. 'I thought not.' His mouth twisted. 'And I suppose your bed is all rumpled from your lovemaking with Linton too.' His voice hardened even more, ripping the robe from her altogether, her skin very pale in the warm light of a summer evening. 'Well, that needn't bother us,' he rasped. 'Because I don't intend going as far as the bedroom, I'm going to take you right here on the floor!'

CHAPTER SEVEN

SHE cowered away from the savage intent in his eyes
not knowing him in this mood. This man was inten'
only on inflicting pain and retribution for a wrong he
believed she had done him with Brian. She had to
make him see sense before he did something they
would both regret.

'Jared, please, you're making a mistake——'

'No, *you* did that, the moment you took me to be a
simple fool!' All the time he was talking he wa'
ripping off his own clothes, first his shirt, his ches'
bronzed, fine copper-coloured hair covering the
darkened skin, next came his denims and the navy
blue underpants, and he stood before her now a'
naked as she was herself, feeling no embarrassment
his body lean and firmly muscled. And even now hi'
arousal couldn't be denied! 'I told you once not to
judge by appearances,' he told her grimly as he pulled
her roughly up against him, the hardness of his body
bruising against her softer curves. 'But you chose no'
to listen,' he ground out. 'Just because I've been
indulgent with you, allowed you a certain amount of
freedom, it doesn't mean I'm stupid——'

'Indulgent? *Allowed* me freedom?' Kate knew that
this was no time for her own anger, that gentle
persuasion was likely to calm him down quicker, and
yet she couldn't help her indignant reaction to his
arrogance. 'You *are* a fool, Jared, if you think you
allowed me anything!' Gone was the need to tell him of
her decision to break her engagement to Richard, to
give the budding love she felt for him, Jared, a chance
to flower and grow, and in their place was a fury that

almost matched his own in intensity. 'I've always done exactly what *I* wanted, when *I* wanted!'

'Then let's hope you want to lie on the floor and accept my body into yours,' he bit out fiercely. 'Because right now that's exactly what's going to happen to you!'

'I won't let you——'

'You won't stop me,' he hissed, his eyes glittering, easily picking her up in his arms to lay her on the carpeted floor, covering her body with his own as she threshed about beneath him in an effort to escape, pinning her arms above her head with just one of his hands, the other one moving to cup her breast, his breathing becoming ragged as his passion increased. 'Your nipples fascinate me,' he groaned as he slid down her body to kiss first one then the other of them, his thumb stroking across the hardening tip. 'A dark dusky red,' he murmured appreciatively. 'And they react instinctively to my caress,' he said with satisfaction as the taut nipples perked enticingly for his pleasure-giving mouth.

Kate knew exactly how the *whole* of her body reacted to his caresses, as she felt that familiar warmth beginning to spread through her body, already her hips wanting to arch against his.

'You see,' he continued to kiss her throat, 'you may have thought you were using me to get back at Linton when we were at the hotel, but you enjoyed it too much for it to be just that. It doesn't take two days of being constantly in bed with a man to take revenge on another one,' he taunted. 'Just the once would have done!'

She could see the truth of his words, knew he was right, she had enjoyed being with him then, but her bitterness had blinded her to that fact.

She gasped as she felt the hot moistness of his tongue encircling her engorged nipple, and tiny rivulets of pleasure shuddered through her body at each tormenting caress.

'You promised yourself you wouldn't do this,' she reminded him desperately, fighting to free her hands as he kissed further down her body, her navel having the full attention of his administrations now, his tongue probing the silken hollow.

'That was to a different Kate,' he rasped.

'I shall hate you!'

Jared ceased the torment of his mouth for a moment as he gave a harsh shout of laughter, moving to look down at her, 'Hate away, Kate,' he taunted, 'but I shall possess your loveliness once more. It's haunted me for long enough!'

'You might possess my body, but you won't possess me!' she groaned as his lips travelled down over the flatness of her stomach.

His eyes were contemptuous as he raised his head to meet her gaze down the length of her body. 'Then I shall possess the only part of you worth having,' he scorned. 'And don't worry about being unfaithful to your fiancé,' he jeered. 'Rumour has it that Richard is in Paris with the lovely Madeleine Duval. You know about her?'

She knew the other woman, one of Richard's French designers, had once been his mistress too. It hadn't occurred to her that he would see Madelaine while he was away. It didn't matter to her now that she did think of it. 'It makes no difference if I do——'

'Of course it doesn't,' Jared's mouth twisted. 'You have Linton, don't you? And now you're going to have me too!'

He was past reasoning with, she could see that, and she knew she had to accept his strength over hers, crying out her heated desire as his gentle caresses continued remorselessly.

She shouldn't be reacting this way to an aggressor,

to a man who was forcing her to respond, to a man who would allow her no respite until she lay in mindless desire as spasms of pleasure ripped through her body. She shouldn't be, but she couldn't stop him!

He loomed over her now, his face as dark as that of the devil, satisfaction at her uncontrollable response to him gleaming from the deep blue eyes. 'Are you tamed yet, wildcat?' he mocked.

Her breath came in short gasps as she sought for normality, hating his lovemaking and yet unable to stop it. 'I hate you!' she spat the words at him.

He gave a wolfish grin, his free hand roaming down the length of her, lingering over the moist warmth of her body, resisting her efforts to hide it from him. 'I can see that.' His taunting gaze returned to her flushed face, darkening suddenly, his mouth tightening grimly. 'I'm going to take you now,' he told her coldly. 'Scratch and claw all you want, it won't stop me. Nothing will do that now.'

Scratching and clawing was all she could do as he released her hands to rest his body between her parted thighs, then possessing her with a fierceness that made her gasp. Her nails raked down his back, she heard him groan as she inflicted the pain, feeling a rough bite to her shoulder as her fingers dug into his buttocks like talons.

'Did you do this to Linton too?' Jared rasped. 'Did you drive him insane too as you gave him pleasure and pain at one and the same time?' His ragged breathing burnt her throat.

Nothing like this had ever happened with Brian, this wild thrill of excitement that couldn't be denied even though she wanted to. Instead she remained silent.

With a furious groan Jared drove into her more fiercely than ever, his hands beneath her holding her into him as she tried to lie impassive beneath him. Denial was impossible, for either of them, and as their bodies reached ecstasy in unison Kate knew that her movements had matched his own thrusting ones, that she had met and equalled his fierce possession.

He lay above her, breathing deeply into her hair, their bodies slicked together with a perspiration of their own making, their thighs still joined, their legs entangled.

It wasn't the time for the doorbell to ring, its shrill ringing bringing with it stark reality. Kate became aware of the carpet beneath her back, the lounge furniture that surrounded them, the sunlight shining brightly through the window on the far wall of the room.

She would have liked to call what had just happened between them rape, and yet she knew it hadn't been. Even in his blazing fury Jared had only shown her ecstasy, had made no effort to hurt her, only to pleasure her. And if that were her punishment then she wanted it to go on and on.

'Your visitor is persistent,' Jared groaned, leaving her as the doorbell rang once again, standing up to pull her effortlessly to her feet. 'I should go and answer it.' He picked up her robe and threw it at her, collecting up his own scattered clothing to walk to the spare bedroom. 'But if it's Linton come back for more I would advise you to get rid of him,' he drawled derisively. 'I have no intention of waiting in the bedroom all night while you conclude your—business with him.' He closed the bedroom door with a decisive click.

Kate felt her anger return at his scathing comments, as she pulled on her robe to fasten the belt with shaking fingers, checking her appearance in the mirror before she went to answer the door. Heavens, was that really her reflected there! Her hair was a tangled mess about her face and shoulders, her eyes a deep languorous gold, her mouth full and swollen from Jared's heated kisses.

She glared at the closed flat door as the bell rang yet again; whoever her visitor was they weren't going to go away. She hurried to the bathroom to quickly wash her face and brush her hair, at least restoring some normality to the chaos Jared's lips and hands had caused.

Gill was just turning away as Kate opened the door, but she turned back gratefully once she saw her. 'Thank goodness!' she sighed her relief, her arms weighed down with heavy vegetable dishes. 'I thought you must be in, you usually are this time of day, and I didn't relish the thought of carrying these upstairs again later tonight. I'm not disturbing you, am I?'

Kate glanced fleetingly at the spare bedroom door, knowing the reason Jared had chosen to use that room to dress, knowing he still believed her bed to show the imprint of her time in Brian's arms. She stepped forward to take some of the dishes from Gill as they unbalanced precariously in her arms. The last thing she wanted was broken vegetable dishes on her doorstep when she had waited this long to have them returned! Besides, the longer Jared spent in the bedroom the more chance of him calming down.

'Not at all.' She led the way into the flat, selfconsciously checking the floor for any article of clothing that might give away the tumultuous lovemaking that had just taken place there. There wasn't one; Jared had not missed a thing. 'Please come through to the kitchen,' she invited woodenly.

Gill put the dishes and their lids down on the table with some relief. 'I don't know how you manage to keep your kitchen so neat and tidy,' she said ruefully. 'Mine always looks such a mess!'

Kate's smile was tight. 'I'm not here often enough to cause a mess.'

The other girl nodded. 'Of course, you just got

engaged, didn't you?' she said wistfully. 'I wish I could get married,' she sighed.

'Perhaps Giles . . .' Kate tidied away the dishes, only half of her attention on Gill, the other half listening in case Jared should leave.

'No,' Gill laughed dismissively. 'Giles' interest doesn't lie in marriage. I——' she broke off as Jared strolled into the kitchen, her eyes widening with appreciation of his lithe attractiveness.

Kate didn't know which one she was more angry with, Gill for instantly falling under the spell of Jared's rugged attraction, or Jared for walking in here looking for all the world as if nothing had happened between them only five minutes earlier, his hair neatly brushed, his worn denims and shirt fitting him easily, none of their earlier passion evident in the coolness of his eyes. At least, they were cool when they looked at her; Gill was a different matter!

Interest kindled in the deep blue eyes as his gaze roamed lazily over the other girl. 'You must be Gill,' he drawled softly. 'I've heard a lot about you.'

'You have?' she breathed huskily, obviously captivated.

'You live downstairs, don't you?'

'That's right.' Wide blue eyes devoured him.

He nodded. 'So Kate told me.' He finally turned to look at her, his expression withdrawn. 'I'm leaving now,' he told her abruptly.

'But——'

'Thanks for the use of the—facilities,' he bit out roughly, silencing her. 'I'll see you again if I come back to town, but Richard should be back soon to take care of you.' He turned back to Gill. 'Nice to have met you.' His tone was at once softer, the smile he bestowed on the other girl completely charming.

Which was more than could be said for the last look

he gave Kate, his eyes steely, his mouth a taut angry line. He was still furious with her!

She turned away, blinking back the tears as she stared sightlessly out of the window. Seconds later she heard the flat door quietly close.

'I *was* disturbing you,' Gill said regretfully. 'I didn't realise you had company . . .'

'I didn't.' Kate hastily wiped away any evidence of tears before she turned back. 'Jared is—He's my brother,' she desperately used the relationship he had claimed several times in the past. 'He's just been staying here for a few days,' she explained.

'Oh,' Gill looked thoughtful. 'I can see the resemblance,' she nodded.

'You can?' Kate looked slightly dazed.

'You have red hair, and your brother's has that deep copper colour,' Gill pointed out. 'Red hair usually runs in a family, doesn't it?' she chattered on.

It could also account for the fact that they both had volatile tempers! Jared could now add a third occasion to the list of when he had completely lost control over his actions, his temper rocketing out of its normal bounds, this time forcing a woman to accept—and like—his lovemaking.

'I didn't realise you had a brother,' Gill continued, not noticing Kate's silence.

'He doesn't come to London very often,' Kate evaded.

'It must have been nice having his company while your fiancé is away,' the other girl nodded.

'Richard is in France for a few days,' Kate confirmed absently, suddenly remembering what Jared had told her about Richard's visit to Paris. Could it really be true that Richard had resumed his affair with the beautiful Frenchwoman he had told her was once his mistress, or had that just been a jealous accusation on Jared's part? Rumour, he had said it was, but Jared's contacts seemed to give him pretty reliable information.

'It must be nice to travel,' Gill said longingly, making herself comfortable on one of the breakfast stools. 'I suppose you'll go with him once you're married, won't you?'

She seemed to be settling herself down for a lengthy visit! 'We haven't really discussed it,' Kate replied awkwardly, thinking of the incongruousness of carrying out such an inane conversation when only minutes earlier Jared had forced her into the joy of his lovemaking. Her legs still felt weak, her body trembling slightly from the fierce tenderness of his caresses.

'I suppose it's too soon yet,' Gill nodded thoughtfully, her chin resting in her cupped hands, her elbows resting on the breakfast bar for support.

'Yes. Er—would you like a cup of coffee?' Kate offered as the other girl seemed in no hurry to leave for a while.

'Thanks,' Gill accepted with a friendly smile. 'I'll make it if you like, maybe you'd like to finish your shower or something?'

'I've already taken my shower,' although it seemed a very long time ago now! 'But I would like to get dressed,' Kate agreed softly.

'Fine,' Gill nodded. 'I'll just make the coffee.'

In the end she stayed for over an hour, something she had never done before, although by the way she poured her heart out about her feelings for Giles, those feelings obviously weren't as deeply reciprocated. Like her, Gill didn't seem to have many close female friends, and Kate had the feeling that the other girl had just needed to talk to someone. Maybe if she had done the same thing after her break-up with Brian she would have got all the bitterness out of her system and could have related to Jared in a normal way at the hotel, wouldn't have stupidly got herself engaged to Richard on the rebound.

When Gill finally left the flat seemed very empty, its clean tidiness showing no signs of the heated scenes that had taken place here tonight, first with Brian, and then with Jared—although the latter had been far more dangerous. She had no doubt that he had gone out of her life for good this time, his disgust as he left had been plain to see.

Nevertheless, she scrambled to answer the telephone when it rang, and her disappointment was acute as she recognised Beryl's voice.

'No personal calls for you, I'm afraid,' Beryl reported regretfully. 'Not even from Richard!'

Somehow Kate wasn't expecting to hear from Richard while he was away, especially after what Jared had told her about Madeleine Duval. And Jared didn't need to telephone her, he had called personally.

'Never mind,' she dismissed lightly. 'Any urgent calls?'

'Mr Harkness wants you to go in tomorrow afternoon to sign the contract.'

'Fine.' Kate couldn't even summon any enthusiasm for that.

'Are you all right, Kate?' Beryl asked concernedly. 'Only you don't sound your usual self.'

She laughed softly. 'I haven't eaten yet.'

'Ah, well that accounts for it,' the other woman laughed. Kate's temper was notorious when she was hungry. 'Tom's chafing at the nosebag too,' she added. 'I'd better get into the kitchen and cook his dinner.'

'Thanks for calling, Beryl. I appreciate it.'

'My pleasure, love. I'll see you tomorrow, hmm?'

All Kate's tomorrows stretched out bleakly in front of her, long empty days and nights without Jared. It was a bitter and empty prospect.

She didn't bother with dinner, not in the least hungry, moving restlessly about the flat, staring moodily out over London, watching the people in the street below her as they rushed home or out, all seeming to have somewhere or someone to go to. She had nowhere she wanted to go, and no one to go with, not if she couldn't have Jared. Somehow, somewhere, she had fallen in love with her blue-eyed devil. Although she had fought admitting it and had constantly denied it to herself and him.

Well, she wasn't denying it now, the full agony of loving a man who no longer loved her was with her, painfully, absolutely. And the pain of it was so much worse than when she had lost Brian. Her love for him had been the love of an adolescent, a youthful destructive love, whereas the feelings she had for Jared were those of a woman, her pain all the harder to bear because she knew she had driven him away with her bitterness and ambition. What did any of that matter, what did the rest of her life matter, now that Jared was gone?

Her sleep was full of hundreds of Jareds, all leaving her, their eyes full of contempt, pushing her away as she would have tried to stop them. And then the old Jared was there, the Jared she had first known, with his laughing blue eyes and gentle hands, soothing her, holding her, telling her he loved her.

And she clung to him, not wanting him to go again, the tears streaming down her cheeks.

'Don't cry, darling,' he groaned. 'For God's sake, don't cry! I won't hurt you again, I promise. Kate!'

Her lids flew open, staring up at Jared in the darkness. It was no dream. Jared lay in the bed beside her, his bronzed bare chest visible above the bedclothes as he held her in his arms, his face agonised as he looked down at her.

'Don't cry,' he smoothed away her tears. 'Darling, please don't cry any more,' he moaned shakily.

He really was here, the man that she loved, the tender lover, his anger gone, and love for her shining in his deep blue eyes.

CHAPTER EIGHT

'JARED ...' Kate breathed her ecstasy, her hands clutching desperately at his broad shoulders, determined he shouldn't escape her now that he had come back, not caring how he came to be here, or of their anger earlier, only knowing she wasn't going to let him leave her again, not until he knew she loved him.

His dark head was bent as he kissed the curve of her throat, the deep swell of her breasts, his body arched over her as one of his legs pinned her beneath him, his proximity telling her of his aroused nakedness. 'I couldn't leave things like that between us, Kate,' he told her shakily, looking down at her intently, 'Ugly.' His mouth twisted. 'I know I hurt you, that you hate me now. But I can't bear your last memory of me to be my brutality.'

'Last memory?' she repeated sharply, tensing in panic. 'Jared——?'

'After tonight I swear to you I'll leave you alone, leave you to live your life the way you've chosen.' He framed her face with his large gentle hands. 'But I can't—call it pride, arrogance—I can't let you go on remembering only that I raped you. God, if I could undo that I would, but——'

'Jared!' With a burst of strength that left him startled she pushed him over on to his back, her eyes glowing as she looked down at him. 'I'm going to "rape" you in the same way,' she mocked huskily.

He frowned, although the frown soon turned to a low groan as she began to kiss his body, starting with his chest and slowly making her way downwards, each caress, each stroke of her lips building the throbbing desire within him, holding his hands immobile at his sides as he would have stopped her more intimate caresses.

'Rape, Jared?' Once again she looked down into the flushed arousal of his face, his eyes dark with passion, and shook her head slightly. 'Between you and me it can only ever be called making love, I know that now.'

'Kate . . .?'

The look of anguished hope in his face couldn't be misinterpreted, and kissing him deeply, she told him the words she had longed to say but thought she never would. 'I love you, Jared.' It was so easy and beautiful to say, so right and natural. 'Brian was only here because——'

'I'm not interested,' he cut in with dismissal, leaning up on one elbow to search the loving glow of her face, the candour of her eyes that shone with her love for him. 'Yes,' he began to laugh softly, triumphantly. 'Yes, it's true—you do love me! Oh, Kate, Kate!' he crushed her to him. 'I never thought you would say those words to me! Kate . . .' The last came out as a ragged groan, then he captured her lips in a kiss that banished any further talk, their lips and bodies all the communication they needed for the next hour, prolonging their passion, tormenting each other's desire until finally Jared couldn't take the torture any longer, and took her with a swift, devastating passion that had them both crying out their rapture within minutes.

'I think,' Jared remarked long breathless moments later, his face buried in her throat, neither of them prepared to relinquish the joined closeness of their bodies just yet, his hand still idly caressing her from breast to thigh, 'that any close neighbours you have will think you've just been attacked!'

Kate smiled with languorous satisfaction. 'No one seems to be running to my rescue.'

'No,' he drawled acknowledgment of the fact. 'Perhaps it's as well, they're going to have to get used to you being "attacked" a lot in future!'

'Mm, nice,' she murmured appreciatively.

He raised his head to look down into her sleepy face. 'Are you going to fall asleep on me?' he teased.

'You have that the wrong way round,' she mocked, her lids feeling very heavy. 'But yes, I think I am.' She yawned tiredly as if to confirm it.

'We have to talk . . .'

'In the morning, darling.' She touched the hardness of his cheek with loving fingertips, smiling drowsily. 'Nothing else is important except that we love—You didn't say you love me,' she realised in a stricken voice, her eyes wide.

'Because it isn't necessary,' he chided gently. 'I can't *stop* loving you.'

Her smile was back, that satisfied sleepy smile that told him she couldn't stay awake for much longer. 'I love you.' Her eyes closed.

'Say my name,' he groaned close to her ear.

She gave an irritated frown of puzzlement, but her lids really were too heavy to keep them open. 'Jared,' she obeyed.

'Again!'

'Jared, Jared, Jared . . .' She had fallen asleep.

'Why?'

Jared blinked up at her with puzzled blue eyes, the sunshine of early morning filtering through the lemon curtains at the window as he stretched with lazy enjoyment, grinning as his arm 'accidentally' brushed against the bared breasts above him. 'Why what?' he asked in a preoccupied voice, turning his head to slowly kiss the dusky nipples that so enchanted him.

Kate moved impatiently, wanting to talk now,

needing to talk. 'Why did you make me say your name last night?' she asked quietly. 'Why like that?'

His face darkened, the passion quickly dying from his eyes as he looked at her unsmiling face, sensing the tension in her. 'Kate——'

'Was it because you didn't think I knew who you were?' she rasped.

'Darling——'

'It was,' she realised flatly. She had woken with the knowledge that Jared had issued that last instruction for a reason, and as she lay beside him for the last hour waiting for him to wake up she had known what that reason was; he truly believed she hadn't known the name of her lover! She could see the truth of that now in his face as consternation washed over him. 'We'd just made beautiful love together and you didn't think I knew *who* you were?' Her anger was obvious, her eyes flashing like molten gold.

'Darling, it wasn't like that——'

'Wasn't it?' she scorned. 'I happen to think it was! God, I offered then to tell you about Brian, but you didn't want to listen. Now I don't know if I should tell you anything! You didn't say my name either at the end, you know,' she snapped. 'I could have been any one of those women you——' Jared's hand gently but forcibly over her mouth silenced her.

'I love you, Katharine Mary Collier,' he told her throatily. 'And I'm sorry if anything I said last night hurt you. I didn't mean it to.'

'No?' She wasn't mollified.

'Darling, please let's not argue,' he cajoled as she still burned with anger. 'We're together now, isn't that all that's important?'

'Why did you came back last night?'

'I couldn't stay away,' he told her simply.

'And just *how* did you get in here?' she frowned.

He grinned. 'The same way as last time—Ben. I told

him I'd been telephoning you for hours but could get no answer, that I was worried about you. He let me in, I checked that you were safely asleep in your bed, assured him you wouldn't mind my staying the night in your spare room, and then——'

'Proceeded to wake me up,' she put in dryly. 'I really must have a serious talk with Ben, he can't keep letting strange men into my flat!'

Jared moved with a swiftness that left her breathless, above her before she knew what he was doing, pinning her beneath him. 'Strange *man*,' he corrected fiercely.

'I'm glad you can admit it,' she mocked, her eyes full of mischief.

'Tormenting woman!' he grimaced. 'But I'm sure Ben wouldn't have let me in if he weren't still convinced I'm your brother.'

'Gill thinks the same thing too now. Well, I could hardly tell her you're my lover after the cold way you left earlier,' Kate told him irritably as he frowned, pushing him away from her, swinging her legs out of bed to stand up, pulling on her robe and securing it tightly. 'I think we should talk now, Jared,' she avoided his troubled gaze. 'And I can't even think straight when you're near me like that.'

'Do you have to?' he groaned, falling back against the pillows, his arm thrown back over his head.

'Yes, I have to.' She moved forward to callously pull back the bedclothes, forcing herself not to be affected by the smooth, lean beauty of him. 'I'll go and make some coffee.' She walked calmly to the door. 'Join me in the lounge when you're dressed.'

'Yes, ma'am,' he drawled, looking at her with mocking eyes.

She gave a mocking laugh, although her laughter faded as she made her way to the kitchen. The way they had made love might have solved a lot of the problems between them, but they still had a lot to sort out, not least of all Jared's distrust of her. She might have accepted his excuses a few minutes ago, but his lack of faith in her still rankled. They had a lot of talking to do today, a lot of decisions to be made on her part.

She was sitting on the sofa when Jared came out of the bathroom to join her, his hair still damp from his shower, his black shirt and trousers moulded to the muscular contours of his body.

He rubbed his jaw ruefully as he sat opposite her, the growth of beard there rasping against his hand. 'You don't appear to have a razor I could use,' he grimaced.

'In the bedroom.' She sipped her coffee, pushing the other mug across the tray towards him. 'It's electric,' she explained.

'With your permission I'll use it later,' he nodded.

Kate eyed him curiously. 'Where are your own things?'

'At—at a friend's.' He seemed to amend his first frank reply. 'Shall I collect them later?'

Her head went back at his evasion. 'We'll have to see, won't we?' She sighed, putting down her half empty mug of coffee. 'First I think I should tell you why Brian was here last night.'

'I told you, that isn't necessary,' Jared said tightly, suddenly giving her a sharp look. 'Unless you intend to go on seeing him?'

'No!'

'Then you don't owe me any explanations. I don't have the right to ask for them.'

'I gave you that right last night!' Kate chewed on her bottom lip. 'Brian's visit here was—unexpected.' She sought about in her mind for the right words, an explanation that would satisfy both Jared and herself; there were five years of loyalty to Brian to dispel even now. 'His marriage to Coral is in difficulty, and he—he——'

'Wants to come back here,' Jared finished tautly.

'Yes.' She flushed her anger. 'But until he turned up here yesterday I hadn't seen him for three months. There's been no affair between him and me behind Coral's and Richard's backs.'

'And now?'

She could sense he believed her, but that her next answer mattered more to him that anything else. And she wanted to be totally honest with him, with herself too. 'At first,' she breathed deeply, 'I felt—pleased that he wasn't happy with Coral, that it was what he deserved, then I felt—I felt saddened that he'd made such a mess of his life.'

'And when he told you he wanted you back?' Jared watched her with hardened eyes, making no effort to drink his cooling coffee.

'Again I felt pleased.' She stared sightlessly across the room at the far wall. 'I—It felt good to know he wanted me again, that he couldn't do without me.'

'I see,' Jared rasped, his voice like gravel.

'No, you *don't*,' she turned fiery eyes on him. 'As he kissed me——'

'*God!*' Jared stood up forcefully, moving to stand in front of the window, his back rigid as he looked out but didn't see.

Kate didn't move, not even looking at him, but staring down at her bare feet. 'He didn't make love to me as you accused last night, but he did kiss me—and all I could think of was that he had no right to do so, that he had made his decision and chosen Coral, and that I didn't want any other man but you to touch me ever again.' Now she did look at him, her love shining in her eyes as he slowly turned to look at her in return. 'It's true, Jared—as he kissed me I knew I couldn't go through with marrying Richard, that it was you I wanted. I finally convinced Brian that I was no longer interested in him, and when he'd gone I realised it was you I was in love with.'

'And then I stormed in ranting and raving like a lunatic,' he groaned, very pale beneath his tan. 'God, what must you have thought of me?'

'I thought that all I wanted was for you to come back to me,' Kate admitted with frank honesty.

'Even after I—after I——'

A wan smile curved her lips. 'I thought we'd settled that last night. We might have been a little rough with each other, but the result was still the same, beautiful pleasure. Besides,' her smile deepened, 'I may have a few bruises to show for last night, but I seem to remember seeing some nasty scratch marks down your back this morning.'

'War wounds,' Jared shrugged. 'Are you really going to break your engagement to Richard?' He sounded anxious.

She nodded. 'As soon as he gets back from France.'

'What I said last night about him and Madeleine Duval didn't influence your decision at all, did it?'

'No,' she lightly dismissed his anxiety. 'Although if it is true it could make things easier when I tell him I can't marry him. Is it?'

Jared looked uncomfortable, moving restlessly back across the room with long strides. 'I don't know,' he admitted. 'It could be, he usually spends time with her when he's in Paris.'

'According to rumour,' she mocked dryly.

'Yes,' he grimaced. 'Although he could just as easily be spending all his time working.'

'You bastard!' she said with cheerful indulgence.

He smiled. 'I've had that said to me before.'

'Probably because it's true.' She met his smile with one of her own. 'But I love you, anyway.'

'Thank God for that.' He pulled her into his arms.

'*Now* can I bring my things over here?' He buried his face in her throat.

'I'll come with you to get them if you like.'

'No! Er—no,' he repeated in a calmer voice. 'I'll go over later, when you're at work.'

'A woman, Jared?'

His mouth tightened. 'I told you, no. It's just—you may not approve of my friends.'

'I'm sure I won't,' she agreed lightly. 'And you're right, I do have to get to work now.'

'Right now?' he groaned, his body already aroused as he moulded her curves to his own, his lips caressing her throat.

'Right now,' she nodded, although she was aware her words lacked conviction. 'I'm seeing Colin Harkness later today.'

'How much later?' he growled.

'This afternoon, actually,' she revealed slowly, knowing by the wolfish grin he gave her that he had the perfect way for her to pass the morning. She couldn't imagine anything more perfect herself. 'Aren't you pleased?' Her arms went up about his neck, her fingers lacing in the thick darkness of his hair.

'Aren't you?' he taunted as she arched against him.

Kate laughed huskily. 'You have a grey hair,' she told him impishly, singling out the grey hair at his temple.

'What do you expect?' he said with amusement. 'It's aged me ten years chasing after you!'

She moved out of his arms, her hips swaying with a natural grace as she went to the bedroom. 'You shouldn't have let me escape in the first place,' she turned to tell him impudently, her eyes glowing with mischief.

Jared quickly followed her, closing the door firmly behind them. 'I didn't *let* you do anything.' He deftly unbuttoned his shirt, throwing it uncaringly to the floor. 'You ran out on me,' he remembered grimly, the rest of his clothes quickly followed his shirt.

Kate's breath caught in her throat at the male beauty of him, her hands shaking slightly as she removed her robe to slide beneath the tousled bedclothes, her arms opening in welcome to him as he quickly joined her. 'You could have come after me then,' she murmured, playfully biting his earlobe.

'It would have been better if I had.' His hand sought out her left one, pulling it out into the light of day, his angry gaze fixed on the diamond ring she still wore. 'Then you would never have worn this damned thing. Ever.'

Kate could tell by the vehemence of his tone that he was still deeply angry about her engagement to Richard. 'I'll take it off——'

'No,' he bit out harshly. 'Wear it until you give it back to him. That way I'll know——' he broke off with a groan, kissing her fiercely.

'You still don't trust me, do you, Jared,' she realised as his mouth left hers to rain searing kisses down her throat. 'I *will* finish with Richard, I promise you that. It's you I love.'

'Show me,' he groaned shakily. 'Show me how much you love me, my Katharine Mary.'

She could easily hear the uncertainty in his voice and knew that it was going to take a long time to convince him of her love. And after all the things she had said to him in the past that wasn't surprising! She began to kiss him as if she never wanted to stop.

'I gather he called some time last night,' Beryl remarked early that afternoon, bringing in the mail for Kate to read.

Kate knew that she glowed with an inner happiness, that her eyes shone like the brightest gold, that her mouth had a perpetual curve. But she felt so happy, so much in love that she couldn't seem to stop smiling. When she had left the flat half an hour ago, reluctantly, Jared had still been in bed, declaring he was too exhausted to get up!

'And I didn't mean Richard,' Beryl drawled as she received only a starry-eyed look in reply to her statement.

Some of Kate's exhilaration faded. 'Has he telephoned at all this morning?' A worried frown marred her brow.

'No.'

Relief shuddered through her; she wasn't looking forward to her confrontation with Richard at all.

'I'll be old and grey by the time you put me out of my suspense,' Beryl groaned.

'Sorry.' Kate gave the other woman a bright smile, deciding there would be plenty of time to worry about Richard once he was back from France.

'Well, did he call or didn't he?' Beryl demanded in exasperation.

'Not exactly. He—he came to see me instead,' Kate explained hastily at the other woman's frustrated sigh.

'Oh.'

'Just—oh?' Kate quirked mocking brows.

'Oh,' Beryl nodded. 'And I'm relieved I didn't telephone your flat this morning to see if you were ill,' she grimaced, preparing to leave the office.

'So am I,' Kate grinned. 'A very disgruntled male might have answered!'

'That's what I thought,' her secretary said dryly. 'Don't forget your appointment with Mr Harkness at two o'clock,' she warned on her way out.

As if she could forget it! Kate had been battling with herself for the last hour over whether or not she should inform the dour Mr Harkness that Richard was no longer going to become her husband. The fact that *she* knew he had helped her to get the contract meant that she should really tell the other man, although she hadn't spoken to Richard yet, and he ought to be told first. She also knew that she was capable of doing the job without the backing of Richard's influence. Nevertheless, she felt professionally torn.

In the end the decision was taken out of her hands.

'It's Mr Harkness on the telephone, Kate,' Beryl buzzed through to her office about fifteen minutes later just as Kate was preparing to leave for her appointment with him.

She frowned. 'Put him on,' she replied in a distracted voice. She was supposed to be seeing him in his office across town in twenty minutes, so why bother to call her now? There seemed to be only one answer to that. 'Good afternoon, Mr Harkness,' she greeted him coolly.

'Miss Collier,' he sounded as abrupt as usual, 'I'm afraid I have to cancel our appointment for this afternoon.'

That was what she had been afraid of. 'I see,' she replied guardedly.

'Something has come up that requires my urgent attention, so I'm afraid we'll have to make our appointment for some time next week now.'

Was it her imagination or was that triumph she heard in his voice? 'Monday?' she prompted stiltedly.

'Just a moment.' He seemed to be taking time to consult his diary. 'Not Monday, I'm afraid. Perhaps one day later in the week?'

'When?' she persisted, having been fobbed off enough in the past by this man.

'Let me see,' he murmured thoughtfully. 'Wednesday, four o'clock?'

That was five days away, but it didn't sound as if she had any choice in the matter! 'Wednesday will be fine,' she accepted distantly, and rang off with a rueful

sigh. What was that saying, 'Bad news travels fast'? It
certainly seemed to have done so this time. She had
only known herself last night that she would have to
break her engagement to Richard, she would be
interested to know who Colin Harkness's informant
was. Because there could be no other explanation for
this sudden cancellation of their appointment. Colin
Harkness had heard of the precariousness of her
engagement and was waiting to see which way things
went. She was well aware that was the 'something'
that had come up so urgently to prevent Colin
Harkness seeing her this afternoon; she just wished
she had been able to sign the contract first. Whether
Richard was to be her husband or not couldn't detract
from her capabilities.

As she wasn't to go out after all she did her best to
catch up on the work she had neglected this morning,
tidying away promptly at five despite her late start to
the day, needing to pick up a few groceries now that
she had a permanent house-guest.

Jared wasn't at the flat when she arrived home,
although when she went into her bedroom she saw his
case and rucksack on the floor in there, and there was
a smile on her face as she went back to the kitchen to
unpack her shopping.

She had showered and changed into denims and a
loose linen blouse, her hair loose down her back the
way Jared liked it, the chicken in the oven cooking in a
delicious mushroom sauce, when she heard the flat
door close, Jared using the key to get into the flat that
she had given him only that morning.

She ran excitedly out of the kitchen to go and greet
him, stopping in her tracks as she looked at him, at a
Jared she had never seen before. Used to seeing him in
faded denims and equally casual shirts and tee-shirts,
she had some difficulty in assimilating this new Jared
with the old one. A navy blue pin-striped suit, the

waistcoat taut against his flat stomach, a silk shirt beneath this, a navy blue tie knotted meticulously at his throat, the black shoes on his feet looking handmade, were all a little hard to take in, the contrast too much.

'Jared . . .' She stood dazedly in the kitchen doorway, a drainer spoon held uselessly in her hand, forgotten as she had run to meet him.

He seemed to notice her for the first time, for a moment looking as startled as she did. Then he put down the black leather briefcase he had been carrying to come towards her, kissing her warmly on the lips. 'I wasn't expecting you to be home yet,' he murmured against her throat. 'Dinner smells good,' he sniffed appreciatively.

Kate still gaped at him. He was almost a stranger to her dressed like this, his appearance coming as a complete shock to her.

Jared laughed down at her softly as he saw her stunned expression. 'Surprised?' he drawled.

'I—er—yes,' she gulped.

His mouth quirked at her confusion. 'Did you think I always dressed in denims?'

'Well, I—I——'

'You did,' he taunted. 'And who do you think would employ me if I went to interviews dressed like that?'

She blinked. 'Is that where you've been, to an interview?' It would certainly explain why he looked like an executive. She would employ him herself if he came to see her looking like this—even if he didn't have the right qualifications!

'Yes,' he grimaced, putting her away from him. 'The chance of a job came unexpectedly this afternoon. Unfortunately I didn't get it.'

She gave him a sympathetic look. 'Was it an important position?'

He shrugged. 'Not bad.'

'Never mind, darling,' she soothed. 'Why don't you get changed and then we'll have dinner; it's almost ready.'

'Great. Do I have time for a shower first?'

'Of course,' she smiled, arching her brows. 'Aren't you going to unpack your clothes too, they'll crease if you leave them in the case any longer. Especially if you have any more lovely suits like this one,' she teased him.

Jared gave a sheepish smile. 'I have one or two, a remnant of the time I was assistant to the Chairman. I'll be about ten minutes, all right?'

'Fine.' Kate went back into the kitchen to check on their dinner.

'Hell, I almost forgot——' Jared appeared in the doorway. 'How did your meeting with Harkness go?'

Her smile faded, her eyes shading over. 'Can we talk about it over dinner?'

'After it, if you would prefer.' His sharp gaze searched her face.

'I think I would,' she grimaced. 'That way I won't get indigestion.'

'Kate . . .!' Jared took her in his arms, kissing her deeply, soon looking down with satisfaction at her flushed face and glowing eyes. 'Still love me?'

'Of course,' she answered without hesitation, then frowned suddenly. 'Is that why you didn't unpack your clothes, because you thought I might have changed my mind since we parted at lunchtime?' She leant back to look up at him.

He gave a grimace of guilt. 'It was a possibility. Please, don't get angry,' he pleaded hastily as he saw the hurt look in her eyes. 'I just couldn't be sure . . .'

She gently caressed the hardness of one lean cheek. 'You soon will be, darling,' she said softly. 'I'll convince you. I know I can't seem the most reliable of people to fall in love with, but I really do love you.

Maybe after a few years of my telling you that you'll believe me.'

'Maybe,' he nodded abruptly, moving away from her. 'I'd better go and change, the dinner smells too good to ruin.'

'It will be.' Kate joined in his lighter mood, more conscious than ever that he hadn't actually mentioned marriage since she had told him she loved him. Maybe he was just wary of another verbal slap in the face, she had certainly given him enough of them in the past! Oh well, as she said, perhaps they just needed time to be confident of each other's feelings.

Dinner was a complete success. Jared was complimentary about the food she had prepared for him, giving no indication that he had noticed her own lack of appetite as he talked to her teasingly, although Kate felt sure that he had, remembering how astute he had been on other occasions. She felt grateful to him for helping her delay talking of her disappointment about Melfords.

It wasn't until after they had cleared away after the meal and were seated together on the sofa, the lights, dimmed, a softly romantic record on the stereo, that he asked her again about her meeting with Colin Harkness.

Kate looked up at him, lying full length on the sofa, her head resting across his thighs as he sat one end of it, idly playing with a silken tress of her hair as he waited for her answer. 'He cancelled,' she sighed, and turned away, a dejected droop to her mouth. 'Just out of the blue, only twenty minutes before I was to see him, he cancelled.'

'Why?'

She shrugged. 'I have an idea, but—Ouch, Jared, that hurt!' She squirmed around to look at him as he tugged hard on the strand of hair he had twirled around his finger.

'Sorry, darling,' he bent to kiss her temple. 'Sorry,' he muttered again as she protested at being squashed.

Kate frowned, smoothing her hair. 'It doesn't matter,' she shrugged.

'You were telling me about your theory as to why Harkness cancelled,' he reminded her.

'Mm,' her frown deepened, 'I think it has to do with Richard.'

'Richard?' he repeated incredulously.

'There's no need to look so surprised,' she snapped irritably. 'He was the reason Harkness offered me the contract in the first place, you know.'

'He was?'

She gave Jared a suspicious look for his deliberately bland tone. 'Are you laughing at me?'

'Certainly not.' He opened widely innocent blue eyes. 'I just don't understand the workings of a woman's mind that can find some connection between Richard James and Colin Harkness. You said Richard doesn't even know the man,' he shrugged his puzzlement.

'He doesn't, but—I may as well tell you,' she sighed. 'It looks as if everything is going to fall through with this contract anyway. But I don't want you to feel in the least responsible for that——'

'Me?' he cut in dazedly. 'How could I be responsible for your losing the contract?'

Kate grimaced. 'Colin Harkness didn't want me for his company, I could tell that when I first met him, then in the middle of the meeting, just as he was about to politely but firmly tell me he wasn't interested, he got a telephone call. You would have enjoyed seeing it if you know the man, Jared,' her mouth twisted. 'He did everything but get down and grovel on the floor to the caller!' Her expression hardened. 'I think he was told then of my involvement with Richard. And when I told him I was engaged and getting married soon he almost had apoplexy!'

'I see,' Jared said softly. 'So you think it was because you're marrying Richard that you were offered the contract?'

Kate nodded. 'And now that it's somehow been leaked that the engagement might be off——'

'You think the offer of the contract might be withdrawn again,' he finished thoughtfully.

'Yes, but I don't want you to worry about it.' She sat up to put her arms about his neck, kissing him deeply. 'I'm sure I would have realised my mistake before I married Richard even if I didn't love you,' she assured him. 'I just wish I knew how Colin Harkness found out about us now. I don't suppose you accidentally mentioned it to one of your "contacts in the business world"?' she frowned.

He steadily met her gaze. 'Does that question really qualify an answer?' he bit out tautly.

She flushed at the way he had taken her half serious, half teasing question completely seriously. 'No,' she gave him a pleading smile. 'I'm just on edge wondering what's going to happen when I go and see Harkness next Wednesday.'

'Wednesday is a long way off.' Jared moved to stand up, taking her with him, holding her easily in his arms. 'And luckily I have the perfect way to stop you feeling on edge.'

Her arms clung about his neck as he strode into the bedroom. 'You do?' She looked up at him with widely guileless eyes.

'Just leave it all to Dr Rourke.' He laid her gently down on the bed. 'I'll take care of all that tension for you.' His eyes hungrily ate up the beauty of her face. 'God, no man would stand a chance if the seductive quality in you could be bottled and manufactured!' he groaned, coming down on one knee on the bed beside her. 'You're the most beautiful woman I've ever seen,' he told her huskily as his eager hands parted her unbuttoned blouse to reveal her bared breasts. 'I always did think you had too many clothes on, especially here,' he murmured against her breast, taking the taut peak into his lips, pulling gently on the nipple as he sucked it further into the warm cavern of his mouth.

'I've been longing for you all afternoon,' Kate groaned, her fingers lovingly caressing the dark softness of his hair. 'Did you miss me as much as I missed you?'

'More,' he murmured against her navel.

'How can you tell? How do you——'

'Kate,' he looked up at her with reproving eyes, 'there's a time to talk, and there's——'

'—a time not to,' she finished ruefully. 'And I think I just found out the occasion when it's better not to,' she groaned as his hands strayed beneath the denim of her trousers.

'Only just?' he mocked against her earlobe.

'Maybe I just needed to be reminded,' she encouraged throatily.

Jared's method of 'reminding' her left them both exhausted; he was heavy above her, but he seemed not to have the strength to be able to move.

'Have there been a lot of women, Jared?'

His head was raised abruptly. 'What sort of question is that to ask me at a time like this?' he rasped. 'Of course there've been women, I told you that when you asked me about Coral.'

'Did you love any of them?'

He leant on his elbows to take some of his weight off her. 'No.'

Kate looked up at him curiously. 'You sound very sure.'

'I am. That's how I knew when I met you that this time it was going to be different.'

'You knew then?' Her eyes widened.

'Yes,' he grinned. 'Now have you finished probing into my lurid past?'

'I don't know, have I?'

His smile faded. 'For the moment,' he nodded. 'We have plenty of time to discover all there is to know about each other. Right now I'm going out to the lounge to switch off the stereo and turn off the lights, and then I'm going to come back to bed and show you we don't need words to communicate. And we have all weekend to communicate in any way we want to,' he promised throatily.

Kate watched with undisguised pleasure as he walked across the room and went out to the lounge. He was the most beautiful man she had ever seen, and she gave her love unreservedly. The next two days promised to be some of the happiest in her life so far.

But what of the rest of their lives together? She was very much aware that Jared had made no further mention of a legal commitment between them, a commitment she would now be more than happy to make.

CHAPTER NINE

'YES, yes, of course.' Kate's hand tightly gripped the telephone receiver in her hand. 'About eight. I'll be there,' and she rang off.

'Be where?' Jared came through from the bathroom towelling his hair dry, another towel secured about his waist, the copper-coloured hair on his chest curled into damp tendrils against his skin. 'Are you going somewhere?'

Kate's gaze was riveted on him. She had come to know him well during the last two days, loving everything about him with an intensity that shook her. And now their idyll had been shattered, reality intruding into the small but ecstatic world they had made together in her flat.

'What is it?' Jared was instantly alert to her change of mood, the pensive frown to her brow, the troubled look in her eyes, and he came over to join her as she sat on the side of the bed. 'Who was that on the telephone just now?' His arm was about her shoulders in the black silk robe as he held her close against him.

She swallowed hard. 'Richard.'

Jared's arm tightened painfully for a second, then eased. 'Did you tell him about us?' he rasped.

Kate shook her head. 'I didn't think it was fair to tell him that way.' She chewed on her inner lip. 'He called to tell me he'll be back late this afternoon; I've agreed to meet him at his flat tonight.'

Jared's mouth firmed. 'At his home? Is that wise?'

She looked up at him with puzzlement. 'Wise?' she frowned at his choice of word.

He nodded grimly. 'If you were my fiancée about to tell me you couldn't marry me I would react in two ways—I would either grow violent, or I would try to seduce you into changing your mind. Neither of those reactions are ones I'll allow Richard James to show you.'

'Richard isn't like that——'

'All men are like that if something they want looks like escaping their grasp,' he bit out. 'And no man would give you up willingly.'

Kate caressed the rigidity of his cheek. 'I think you're biased, darling,' she teased.

'No.' His eyes were as hard as ice, silver blue. 'You really want to meet him?'

'I don't have any choice, do I?' she reasoned. 'It isn't the sort of thing I could tell him over the telephone.'

'No,' Jared acknowledged abruptly, and stood up. 'Shouldn't you be dressing for work?'

'Jared . . .?'

He turned from taking a chocolate-brown coloured suit out of the wardrobe, his cold expression not encouraging. 'Yes?'

'Darling!' She ran to him, her arms about his waist, her head resting against his chest, his heartbeats sure and strong. 'Darling, it will be all right,' she fervently assured him, looking up at him appealingly. 'I'll just tell Richard I can't marry him and then leave.'

A nerve pulsed erratically in the rigid line of his jaw. 'It won't be that easy,' he warned her tautly.

'Of course it will,' she told him lightly, smiling up at him brightly, looking with interest at the three-piece brown suit he had taken out of the wardrobe to put on. 'Do you have another interview today?'

'Interview? Oh—oh yes,' he nodded distantly.

'Important?'

'It could be.'

'Aren't you going to tell me about it?' She quirked darkly auburn brows.

He shrugged. 'Maybe when I get back.'

Kate could see her effort to change the subject and talk him out of his dark mood wasn't going to work, the tension in him a tangible thing. 'Okay,' she accepted softly. 'We'd better get dressed, then, hadn't we? Neither of us wants to be late.'

Again the unfamiliar figure of Jared in a formal suit stunned her for several minutes when she came back to their bedroom after her shower. There was no other word for it, he looked devastating!

'Is the person doing the interview a woman?' she teased as she began to dress.

He arched dark brows. 'Why?'

'Because if she is you already have the job,' Kate drawled.

'Now, now!' he tapped her playfully on the nose. 'That's called jealousy,' he smiled.

'If by that you mean I'd like to hit every woman who looks at you and wants to go to bed with you, then I agree!' Her eyes glittered in challenge of any woman daring to even think such a thing about Jared.

His arms tightened about her, curving her body into his. 'Do you want to go to bed with me when you look at me?' he mocked.

'All the time!' she groaned, her knees already feeling weak from just this contact with him. 'Oh, Jared, do you have to leave just yet?' Her arms curled about his neck. 'Couldn't you miss this one interview and make love to me instead?'

With a hard kiss on the mouth he had released her, turning to pick up his briefcase. 'No, I don't think so,' he said slowly. 'Not this one.'

'What do you have in that thing?' Kate taunted the briefcase in his hand to hide her disappointment, aware that for the first time since she had confessed her love for him Jared had rejected her desire to make love. His appetite had more than matched hers the last two days; they had not even ventured out of the flat for fresh groceries, surviving on what little she had bought on Friday evening whenever they felt hungry, which was often, the two of them finding they had a good appetite for food once they had made love. 'Your lunch?' she scorned him.

His mouth curved into a tight smile at her humour, although his eyes remained hard. 'It looks good, gives people the impression I'm a capable businessman.'

'Yes, but what does it have in it?' She tried to take it out of his hands, but he refused to release it. 'Jared?' she frowned at his set expression.

'It's empty,' he told her flatly.

'It didn't feel emtpy . . .'

'So I do have a couple of sandwiches in there for my lunch,' he acknowledged lightly. 'I thought you'd be angry; I took the last of the bread.'

'It doesn't matter,' she dismissed in a preoccupied voice. 'I'll get some more on the way home tonight. Jared, you are going to an interview, aren't you?' Concern edged her voice.

'Of course.' Deep blue eyes searched her worried face. 'What do you think I'm going to do, rob a bank?' he mocked the claim he had once made over buying her roses. 'Smuggling drugs out of the country——'

'Nothing that serious——'

'But something illegal, hmm?' he scoffed. 'Really, Katharine Mary, what a suspicious mind you have!'

'I just don't want you to think you have to go out and make money——'

'Any way I can,' he put in tauntingly.

Kate shot him an irritated glance. '—just to try and prove something to me,' she finished tightly. 'As far as I'm concerned you don't have to get another job, ever, if you don't want to.'

'Just laze around while you go out to work, hm?' he drawled. 'I couldn't do that, Kate.'

She had known that already, knew that he was basically a hardworking person, he just didn't see any reason to overdo it. 'All right,' she gave a strained smile. 'But you will—you will be careful, won't you?'

'At an interview, Kate?' Jared mocked. 'How could I be anything else!' He bent to kiss her lingeringly on the lips, his free hand cupping her chin. 'I'll see you tonight,' he said briskly. 'Don't work too hard.'

'I won't.' She watched him as he walked over to the door. 'Good luck.'

'Hm? Oh—thanks.' He gave her a warm smile before leaving.

A worried frown drew Kate's brows together over troubled golden eyes. She really doubted that Jared had an interview today, or if he did it was for something he knew she wouldn't approve of. Or maybe he just didn't want to get his hopes up in case he didn't get it—although he hadn't seemed too disappointed when he hadn't been successful with the other job on Friday. Heavens, she really hoped he wasn't going to do anything stupid just to prove himself to her. It would be a waste of time, he had already more than proved his worth to her; he meant everything to her.

Her happiness obviously showed as she drove to work, a couple of taxi drivers giving her a cheery wave, the attendent of the underground car park giving her a friendly smile in answer to her bright one. 'Smile and the world smiles with you' seemed to be applicable today. And she couldn't seem to stop smiling. Beryl gave her an indulgent look as she passed through the main open-plan office to her own.

'Have a good weekend?' Kate greeted her secretary cheerfully.

Beryl nodded. 'Did you?' she asked needlessly.

Her mouth quirked. 'Couldn't have been better.'

'That's what I thought,' Beryl said dryly.

Kate laughed with the sheer happiness of being alive and being loved by such a wonderful man as Jared, and she went through to start her work with less willingness than usual; she would much rather have spent the day with Jared. But the fact that he had gone out too made up for that a little, and after some reluctance on her part for the first hour or so she soon settled down to her work with her usual interest.

'Delivery for Miss Collier,' Beryl teased shortly before lunch as she came in with a huge bouquet of red roses. 'Sorry, he didn't deliver them himself this time,' she mocked as she laid the Cellophane-wrapped blooms on the desktop. 'But I'm sure the sentiment is still the same!'

Kate gave her a glowing smile and ripped open the tiny white envelope that contained the card. 'I love you', it read. There was no signature, but then she didn't need one.

'Dare I say this looks serious?' Beryl said half teasingly, half questioningly.

'You dare,' Kate answered in a preoccupied voice, admiring the beautiful roses. 'Because it is,' she looked up to smile ecstatically. 'I love him.'

'And Richard?'

Her smile wavered and faded. She had tried not to think of Richard the last two days, and with Jared filling her senses as well as her mind that hadn't been too difficult to do. But with Richard's call this morning that had all ended, and now she feared for Jared. If by breaking her engagement she lost the Melford contract she could survive, the agency could survive, it always had, but if Richard should find out about Jared, about her involvement with him, then he could use his considerable influence to stop Jared getting another job, ever. But Richard had always been good to her in the past, perhaps he would understand. And perhaps he wouldn't! Oh dear, she didn't know what was going to happen tonight, she only hoped Jared didn't get hurt.

'Kate?' Beryl prompted concernedly at her prolonged silence.

Kate gave her friend a taut smile. 'As you've probably realised, I can no longer marry Richard.'

'You're going to marry Jared.' The other woman sounded pleased.

'Well ...' Kate flushed, 'not exactly. He hasn't asked me.' Lately.

'He will,' Beryl said confidently. 'You just wait and see. Do you want me to put these roses in a vase outside?' she asked tongue-in-cheek.

'Don't you dare!' came Kate's predictable answer.

But a pensive frown marred her brow as she arranged the three dozen red roses into a vase. In the length of that short conversation she had had with Beryl the other woman had mentioned the two subjects that troubled her the most, breaking her engagement to Richard, and the fact that Jared still hadn't mentioned the subject of marriage to her. Not that she wasn't perfectly happy as they were now, she just didn't understand why he suddenly didn't talk of marriage any more.

But she had no doubt that he loved her, and that was all that mattered. If she told herself that long enough she might actually come to believe it! But there was nothing wrong with wanting to be married to the man she loved, her trouble was she had intended being the wife of two men she *didn't* love. No wonder Jared was wary of asking her to make a commitment to him!

She called the flat to thank him for the roses once she had put the vase on her desk. There was no answer, so she assumed he must still be out at his interview. It must be some job if the interview was lasting all day!

She went to the shops after work, getting in enough food to last them a week. At least if they decided to become hermits again they would have enough food this time!

It was lucky she had decided on steaks and salad for dinner, for Jared still wasn't back when she got in at six-thirty. Once again she had showered and changed when she heard his key in the lock, going out to meet him. He looked tired tonight, lines of strain about his eyes and mouth. He threw the briefcase down on the hall table, running a weary hand about the back of his neck.

'Had a hard day, darling?' Kate moved to join him, looking up at him anxiously.

His smile seemed rather forced. 'Not really. How was yours?'

'Fine,' she dismissed. 'Thank you for the roses,' she smiled shyly.

'My pleasure,' he nodded abruptly.

'Jared, what's wrong?' she frowned, sensing the tension in him like a coiled spring.

'Wrong?' He moved to the bottle of whisky she had bought for him today and put on the sideboard with a tray of glasses, Jared having told her he liked a glass of whisky after dinner in preference to the brandy she already had. But it wasn't after dinner yet, and Jared had already downed one glassful of whisky without seeming to feel any effect from it, and was in the process of pouring himself another one. 'Nothing is wrong,' he rasped. 'Not a damn thing!' he scowled, moving forcefully away from her to pace the room. 'Not a thing,' he repeated in a muttered voice, his expression grim.

'Jared?'

His eyes glittered furiously at the uncertainty in her

voice. 'Everything I want for my future could come crashing down about my ears tonight—and you ask me what's wrong!' He drank the last of his whisky, slamming the glass down. 'Every damn thing is wrong—and I can't do a thing to stop it!'

She had never seen Jared in this utterly defeatist mood before. She had seen him teasing, happy, angry, *furiously* angry, but she had never known him to give up on anything. She couldn't imagine what had happened to cause it now.

'Do you have dinner cooking?' he scowled at her with baleful eyes.

'No.' She looked startled by the question. 'I was waiting for you to come home before I——'

'Good.' He grasped her hand and pulled her towards the bedroom.

'Jared, what——'

'You're mine, do you hear,' he told her roughly. 'Mine! I'll never let you go now. Never!'

Kate tried to collect her thoughts as he shook her. 'Of course I'm yours, darling,' she reassured him soothingly. 'I always will be,' she quivered, unnerved by the dangerous glitter in his eyes.

'Will you?' he derided bitterly.

'Of course,' she nodded frantically.

'How can you be sure?' he rasped, pushing her away from him. 'You could see Richard tonight and he could persuade you that you're making a mistake, that you would be a fool not to marry him.'

Kate's eyes widened and she gasped her disbelief. 'Is that what all this is about?' she demanded. 'You trust me so little you think I'll take one look at Richard's wealthy lifestyle, consider all that he could give me, and ditch you so fast you won't even have time to pack your things?' She was breathing hard in her anger.

'Yes,' he bit out. 'Yes!'

'Well, thank you very much!' she snapped furiously. 'And what were you going to do just now, drag me off to bed and hope that would convince me you're a better lover than Richard?' She knew by the uncomfortable flush to his lean cheeks that she was right in her supposition. 'Well, I don't know that you are,' she scorned to hide her deep hurt. 'I've never been to bed with Richard, maybe he's as accomplished a lover as you are. And maybe I'll find that out tonight,' she added challengingly. 'Maybe I'll find that out *right now*!' She turned to leave, but the strong grip on her arm stopped her as Jared brought her back round to face him. 'Let me go!' she ordered through stiff lips, the effect ruined by the tears streaming down her cheeks.

All the anger drained out of Jared, leaving him pale and strained. 'God, I hardly know myself when I treat you this way.' His heated gaze searched her pained face. 'I've hurt you again, haven't I?' he groaned. 'Of course I have, damn it,' he chastised himself. 'Everything was fine until you received that telephone call from James this morning,' his eyes narrowed. 'Ever since I've known you were going to see him tonight I've been unable to think of anything else. I love you, Kate, and the thought of losing you now is driving me insane!'

She remained hardened to the pleading for understanding in his voice. 'Maybe you'd like to come with me?' she derided. 'Then you'll know exactly what happens when I meet Richard.'

Her derision hit home; Jared looked very uncomfortable now. 'I'm sorry,' he said softly.

'Sorry?' Kate repeated in a hushed voice. 'Sorry!' Her voice rose angrily. 'Am I to be mistrusted by you for ever for a few months' understandable confusion in my life?' she demanded angrily. 'You seem to be the one who was so certain from the beginning—if you were so certain why did you go to Canada, why leave it three months before deciding you were in love with me?'

'Canada was business——'

'Of course,' she said tightly. 'Well, I wasn't to know you'd come back after three months and expect to pick up where you'd left off, I wasn't to know you'd come back at all!' She turned away from him, breathing deeply, flinching as she felt his hands come to rest on her shoulders.

Jared pulled her back against his body regardless of her struggles. 'I love you, can't you understand that?' he groaned against her temple. 'I love you!'

With a sob she turned into his arms, holding him tightly to her as he pressed her against his lean length. 'I love you too,' she choked.

'Then what are we arguing about?' he attempted to tease.

'You——'

'I'm a fool,' he smiled down at her. 'I thought we'd already agreed on that.'

'I hadn't,' she gave him a watery smile. 'But I do now.'

His smile deepened. 'Are you going to cook dinner or shall I?'

'But . . .?' She looked about them pointedly, the invitation of the bed obvious.

Jared shook his head, leading her gently out of the room and closing the door on the temptation it offered. 'You're right, nothing can be solved that way.'

'Nothing *needs* to be solved,' once again she tried to reassure him, but she could still see the vulnerability in his eyes. 'Look, I'll call Richard and go over and see him now. It's almost time anyway. Then when I get back we can have dinner together,' she encouraged.

'But aren't you hungry?'

Her mouth twisted. 'I don't think either of us would

enjoy our food just now,' she sighed. 'I'll get things sorted out with Richard, and we can eat later.'

Jared nodded slowly. 'Perhaps that would be best.'

'I'll just go and change——'

'Why?' he asked sharply.

'Why?' she repeated with a frown, not understanding him.

'You look fine to me as you are,' he said with quiet suspicion.

'Richard doesn't like denims on a woman——'

'Then he doesn't know what he's missing,' Jared rasped. 'And if you look good to me, the man you're supposed to love, then why should you change to meet some other man?'

Kate gave him an impatient sigh. 'You're just being difficult——'

'You bet I am!' he said harshly. 'When *I* think you look fine why should you need to dress up for some other man?' he repeated tautly. 'A man who you no longer want to marry?'

'Richard is also a client of mine,' she reasoned.

Jared gave a derisive laugh. 'You really think he'll continue to be once you've broken your engagement to him? Or his business friends either, for that matter?'

Kate gave him a startled look. 'You mean that as well as the Melford contract I could lose the others too?' she queried slowly.

'I would say it's a certainty,' he nodded, his eyes narrowed on her shocked face. 'Did you really not realise that?' he scorned hardly.

'But they signed contracts——'

'Which they could no doubt break in a matter of days,' he said dryly. 'And would you really want to force companies to stay with your agency?' he quirked dark brows.

'No, but—Surely Richard wouldn't—*couldn't*——'

'You said he's a powerful man,' Jared reminded her softly.

'But he could ruin me!'

'Yes,' he confirmed.

Kate's mouth tightened, her eyes dark. 'You don't sound very concerned about the fact that I could be out of business by this time tomorrow!'

He shrugged. 'I'm used to being broke.'

'Well, I'm not!' she snapped, glaring at him. 'I worked that business up from nothing, paid my father back in six months the money he gave me to start it with. I *am* that agency,' she declared stubbornly.

'Then it looks as if your choice is going to be harder to make than you think,' Jared told her quietly. 'If you choose Richard you get to be the wife of a rich man, *and* keep your agency successful. If you choose me, all you get is—me.' He gave a rueful shrug.

Then there was no choice, she knew that. She loved Jared, and the thought of not being with him for the rest of her life scared her to death. And yet she hadn't realised she would lose so much—everything, but Jared himself. But looking at him now, loving him, she knew it was worth it.

With a tremulous smile she threw her arms about his neck, to be instantly caught up in his fierce embrace. 'I can't lose you now, Jared,' she told him huskily. 'Not at any price!'

He still looked troubled, as if her answer wasn't quite what he had been expecting. 'Kate, I have something to tell you——'

She kissed him hard on the mouth. 'It will have to wait until I get back.' She moved out of his arms, looking quickly at her wrist-watch as she pulled on a green velvet jacket and picked up her clutch-bag. 'We've been talking so long now that if I don't leave I'm going to be late,' she gave him another quick kiss.

'I'll be back in about an hour at the most.' She gave him a dazzling smile before leaving.

'Kate!'

She turned to blow him a kiss before stepping into the lift. 'I'll see you soon, darling.'

'There's something we have to talk about, that I have to explain to you!'

'We can talk later,' she promised as the lift doors closed and she began her descent.

The drive to Richard's flat passed without incident—or concentration, as she tried to formulate in her mind what she was going to say to him. The truth would be best, of course, but how to approach the matter, that was her problem.

Richard's greeting when he opened the door to her knock was rather cool, although Kate had expected that; they hadn't exactly parted the best of friends. And she was wearing the denims he so disapproved of. What a good start to what promised to be a traumatic meeting at best!

'Drink?' He stood by the vast array of bottles he had in the cabinet, the door already open, as if he had been in the process of pouring himself a drink when she arrived.

'Whisky and ginger, please,' she requested, noticing she didn't get the usual cold comment about 'spoiling the taste of good whisky'. Maybe France had mellowed him, he had certainly seemed cheerful enough when they had spoken together on the telephone this morning—or could the lovely Madeleine Duval have been the reason for that? If she had that could make what Kate had to say a little easier. 'Did you have a good trip?' she asked casually as he handed her her drink before sitting in the chair opposite her, crossing one well-shod foot over the other.

'Very good,' he nodded.

'Did you settle the problem?'

'Yes. And you, what have you been doing since I've been away?' He looked at her with narrowed eyes.

Kate gave a light laugh. 'The same as usual—working,' she shrugged.

'Have you signed with Melford yet?'

'Not yet.' She sipped her drink, avoiding his gaze. 'But I'm still hoping.'

'Yes,' Richard's mouth twisted.

Kate took a deep breath, knowing she couldn't keep delaying the inevitable with this inane politeness. 'Er—Richard, I'd like to talk to you about—about us.'

'Yes?' His gaze sharpened, looking very cool and relaxed in a dark lounge suit and cream-coloured shirt.

She moistened lips that had gone suddenly dry, never having done anything like this before, and not wanting to hurt anyone. 'Before you went away you told me to seriously consider whether or not I'm the sort of wife you want and need,' she said in a rush.

Richard had a watchful look about him now, his eyes were icy slits. 'That's true,' he answered.

'I——' she chewed on her inner lip, 'I don't think I am!' She looked across at him with stricken eyes.

He didn't seem particularly perturbed by what she had just told him, and pursed his lips thoughtfully. 'Indeed?' he drawled.

'No.' Kate shook her head, taking another frantic sip of the whisky and ginger.

He nodded slowly, his expression still calm. 'Then you want to break our engagement?'

'Yes,' she nodded eagerly, putting her glass down to take off the diamond ring. 'Please.' She held it out to him.

Richard ignored the ring lying in her open palm, and moved to pour himself another drink, his expression having hardened when he turned back to her. 'How long have you known him, Kate?' he rasped suddenly, his eyes glacial.

Hot colour flooded her cheeks and then as quickly faded again, leaving her white, her eyes the only colour in her face. 'I——' she moistened her lips again as they seemed too stiff to move. 'What do you mean?'

'Do you think I'm a fool, Kate?' he scorned roughly, the mask of politeness falling away to leave a very angry man. 'I hadn't been back in England more than an hour when I was *informed* of your little affair!'

'Who told you?' Kate gasped, standing up.

'No denial?' he taunted her reaction.

'I—Well——'

'No denial,' his mouth twisted. 'And my informant told me to tell you to be sure to give you her name. It was Coral Linton.'

She should have known! Coral was both vindictive and jealous, a dangerous combination in any woman. 'What makes you think she told you the truth?' she scoffed. 'Coral is married to my ex-fiancé, she would do anything, *say* anything, to try and hurt me.'

Richard nodded abruptly. 'I took that into account, was prepared to give you the benefit of the doubt— until you walked in here tonight,' he bit out. 'Then I knew every word she'd told me was true,' he rasped. 'Besides, I saw him at your flat once, didn't I?'

Kate frowned, startled. 'Did you?'

'The night we became engaged,' he reminded her grimly. 'Of course I didn't realise who he was at the time, but I do now. So answer me, how long have you known him?'

The hand holding out the ring fell back to her side, putting the ring down on the coffee-table, her hands clenched nervously together in front of her. 'Several months,' she murmured in reply.

'Before you even went out with me?' he demanded. 'Before you accepted my marriage proposal?'

'Yes. But——'

'Then why on earth did you *go* out with me?' he demanded furiously.

'Because he went away!' she cried her anguish. 'I didn't think I would ever see him again,' she added in a choked voice. 'I never meant to hurt you, Richard,' she told him softly, appealingly. 'I just didn't realise how I felt about Jared.'

'And how do you feel?' he asked bitterly.

'I love him,' she replied simply.

'You love him,' Richard repeated scornfully. 'But then I don't suppose it's difficult to love a man like that, is it?' His mouth twisted with bitter humour. 'Just how long do you think you'll manage to hold his interest, Kate?' he derided.

She stiffened. 'We love each other.'

'Really?' he gave a mocking laugh. 'And how long do you think that will last?'

'We're going to be married,' she told him with great dignity, never having expected Richard to behave in this mockingly derisive manner.

His humour deepened. 'When?' he taunted.

'I—Well——' she looked confused. 'We haven't actually set the date yet, but——'

'I'll bet you haven't,' he smiled again, a smile without any real humour.

'And what's that supposed to mean?' Her indignation at his mockery returned.

'Oh, nothing.' He sat down with a completely confident air, looking up at her pityingly. 'Except that I'm sure there will never *be* a wedding.'

'You don't know anything about it!' She was becoming angry in the face of his derision. 'You don't know Jared.'

'Has he asked you to marry him?'

'Several times,' she defended.

'Lately?' he taunted.

Kate blushed anew as he hit on the one vulnerable

spot in her relationship with Jared. 'You have no right to insult a man you don't even know!'

'I know *of* him, that's enough,' Richard taunted.

Her eyes widened incredulously. 'What do you know about him?'

'Mainly that he'll never marry you. Men like Melford never fall into the matrimonial trap unless it's with someone of their own kind; it costs too much in settlements otherwise,' he mocked.

Relief flooded through her as she realised he had made some ghastly mistake, that the things he was saying weren't about Jared at all! She gave a light laugh. 'You have it all wrong, Richard——'

'No—*you* do, if you think you mean any more to him than Coral Linton did several years ago, and the hundreds of other women he's taken to his bed over the last few years since he became Chairman of Melfords.'

Coral . . . Coral was the one who had told Richard the identity of Kate's lover. Why would she lie? Why would she need to, when she knew the real identity of the man? None of this made any sense.

'He may manage to keep his name out of the newspapers with his wealth,' Richard continued grimly. 'But most of us have heard all there is to know about him, and after Mrs Linton's call I made it my business to know. The night he came to your flat I didn't recognise him, not in those clothes,' he derided. 'But I suppose when you're worth as much as he is you don't need to dress the part! And the name Rourke threw me for a while too, then I remembered that he had changed his name to Melford to become Chairman of the company after his grandfather's illness. That damned Lamborghini parked outside as if it owned the world was his too, wasn't it.' It was a statement that didn't require an answer. 'I don't suppose he could resist the power under the bonnet—

I've heard that he thrives on power *and* challenge,' Richard scorned. 'His grandfather was a tough old bird, but Rourke beats him hands down,' he shook his head. 'The old man took him under his wing as soon as he left university at twenty-two, made him work his way up through the company until he was his assistant, then he got the shock of his life when the boy turned out to be tougher than even he was!'

The Lamborghini ... Could turn his hand to anything, had even been assistant to the Chairman of a company! Jared had forgotten to mention the fact that his grandfather was that Chairman, and that he now ran that company himself ...

'The old man hit trouble as soon as he tried to get Jared to change his name,' Richard scorned. 'Jacob Melford only had the one daughter, and she married someone by the name of Rourke, of all things! The old boy flew into a rage about that, although he'd accepted the fact by the time his grandson came along. But he refused to hand over the company until he changed his name to Melford.' His mouth quirked derisively. 'Something Jared refused to do. He walked out on the company and his grandfather, went to the States and made his own fortune there. I doubt if he would have come back at all if his grandfather hadn't had a heart attack. The doctor assured Jared that his grandfather was on his deathbed, and so against his better judgment he agreed to change his name and take over Melfords. Am I boring you, Kate?' he mocked hardly.

'No,' she choked. 'Please—go on.'

Richard laughed without any real humour. 'It seemed old Jacob had outwitted him—or thought he had. The old man made a miraculous recovery, was up and about again in a week, ready to run the business with his grandson as he'd planned all along. But Jared kept him out, threatened to go back to America if his grandfather so much as set foot inside the building again.' He turned to Kate with cold eyes. 'You really think he's the sort of man who would seriously offer you marriage?'

CHAPTER TEN

THE hotel was comfortable, although certainly nothing glamorous. Obscure, was the word Kate would have chosen to describe it. If she had thought about it that much—which she didn't. She felt numb, too numb to think of anything but that Jared had been making a fool of her.

She had left Richard's home without completely losing her pride, giving him no idea that she hadn't known the Jared she loved was really Jared Rourke *Melford*! No wonder she had been considered for the Melford contract—through Jared's influence and not Richard's at all. How he must have laughed at her the night she had told him she believed it to be Richard's power in the City that had got her as far in Melfords as she had! That contract had just been a carrot to dangle in front of her nose, an added incentive if she should prove difficult in her seduction. Jared was just another rich man getting his kicks by making fools of other people. And she had finished playing his game; from now on he played strictly alone.

In the meantime she couldn't go back to the flat, not until Jared had gone, and she had exactly the way to make him leave! Picking up the telephone next to the bed, she dialled for an outside line, then rang her home number, doing it quickly before she had time to change her mind. She still loved Jared in spite of everything!

The telephone was picked up after only one ring. 'Hello?' Jared sounded disgruntled.

Kate swallowed hard, her hand shaking as she grasped the receiver. How could he have done this to her, what sort of man was he that he played with people's lives in this way? Richard had said Jared thrived on power and challenge, and that was exactly what she must have been to him. She loved him, had been willing to sacrifice everything she had for the man she thought him to be, and all the time he had been laughing at her, enjoying a new *challenge*.

'Hello?' he repeated irritably at her lack of response to his question. 'Who is that? Kate?' he demanded intensely.

'No need to get excited, Jared,' she drawled mockingly, amazed at how confident she sounded. 'I was just—distracted for a moment,' she dismissed.

'Where are you?' he wanted to know, his voice sharp. 'You said you'd be back within the hour, and that was two hours ago. Where the hell are you?'

'I've hit a little problem,' she told him softly.

'What sort of problem?' he asked warily. 'Kate, where are you?'

'I'm—No, I won't be long, darling,' she had turned slightly away from the telephone as if talking to someone at her side. 'Of course,' she gave a soft laugh.

'Kate?' Jared's voice thundered down the telephone. 'Are you still at Richard's?'

'Yes——'

'Why? You said you were going to tell him how you felt and then leave,' he reminded her tautly. 'Why didn't you?'

'Because I—It happened just the way you thought, Jared, I changed my mind as soon as I saw Richard again,' she told him lightly. 'Being with you the last few days has been wonderful, but I realise now that I've been making a mistake.'

'You're still going to marry Richard James?' he bit out roughly.

'Yes. You see——'

'No, I don't *see* anything,' Jared rasped. 'You love *me*, you wanted to be with *me*!'

'I realise now that there's more to life than enjoying going to bed with someone,' she told him lightly, and heard him swearing and was relieved that she was telling him this over the telephone and not face to face. 'I can't give up everything I've worked for, Jared, not even for someone as charming as you.'

'Kate, there's something I think I should tell you——'

'I have to go, Jared,' she interrupted firmly. 'I would appreciate it if you would move out of my flat before I get back.'

'I'm waiting right here until you get home. I want to talk to you,' he told her grimly.

She hardened her heart even more, more than ever relieved there was this physical distance between them. 'I'm not coming back tonight, Jared. I—I'm staying here, with Richard.'

There was no reply this time, just the slamming of the telephone receiver ringing in her ears. She had expected no other reaction, wanted no other. This way, no matter what came after, she was the one who had said goodbye.

The tears finally began to fall, and once they did she couldn't stop them, falling back on the bed in this small, impersonal hotel room, the hands that covered her face completely bare of all rings.

She was aware of how pale and drawn she looked the next morning as she studied her reflection in the bathroom mirror, her eyes dark with pain, having a bruised look from a night spent alternately cursing and loving Jared in spite of everything.

Now there was a quiet acceptance about her, knowing that it was all over, that by now Jared would have moved back to the expensively secluded apartment he would have in the fashionable part of

London. She didn't for a moment doubt that Richard told her the truth of who Jared was, knew without *being* told that Jared had spent both Friday and yesterday at his office at the Melford building, that his elegant suits had been worn for that reason, that his briefcase, far from being empty, had been full of important business papers that a man who was Chairman of such an important company would need to carry around with him. No doubt Jared had already lost enough working hours at the beginning of the week when he had tried so hard to convince her he was out of work as well as out of a place to stay!

What he had done to her had been cruel and insensitive in the extreme—and it had made no difference to her love for him. But she could no longer be his mistress, not when he had deceived her so badly. If she had known the truth from the beginning, if he had explained that he had no real intention of offering her marriage, then maybe she could have accepted what he did have to give. But that wouldn't have been enough of a challenge for him, he had to make her believe she was falling in love with an out-of-work, over-age hippie!

A telephone call to her flat ten minutes ago, and another one just now, had told her that he had indeed gone from her flat; she had received no answer to either call. It was safe to go back to her home and change for work, intending to keep up the pretence of normality for as long as possible.

The wardrobe was bare of Jared's clothes—even the dirty laundry had gone!—and the bathroom showed no signs of his toiletries that had been in the cabinet with hers for the last three days. Not anywhere in the flat could she find signs of his presence, and yet she could still sense that he had been there, every single thing here reminding her of the happiness they had shared over the weekend.

She hurriedly changed into one of her feminine business suits, deftly applied the make-up that did a lot to hide her pallor from lack of sleep. Nevertheless, Beryl gave her a double-take as she went through, standing up to dazedly follow Kate through to her office.

'Where have you been?' her secretary demanded worriedly.

Kate glanced at her wrist-watch. 'I'm only half an hour late——'

'I didn't mean that,' Beryl dismissed. 'Where were you last night?'

Dull colour stained her cheeks. 'Last night?' she delayed.

The other woman sighed. 'Jared got me out of bed at one o'clock this morning demanding to know if I knew where you were—the last thing I expected was for you to calmly walk in here ready to start work this morning!'

'Did you tell—Of course not,' Kate grimaced. 'You didn't know.' She frowned. 'Why would he bother you? And how did he know where you live?'

'The latter I can answer,' Beryl said dryly. 'The first I was hoping you would be able to tell me. He got my address from Richard.'

'Richard . . .?' Kate swallowed hard. Then Jared knew she had been lying last night, that far from spending the night with Richard, she had given him back his ring and never expected to see him socially again.

'Yes,' the other woman nodded. 'I gathered from what he said that he'd been to see him too.'

'But why?' Kate groaned her consternation, very pale again. 'Why is he bothering?'

'You tell me,' Beryl prompted gently. 'Have you argued, is that it? He seemed very upset when he came to my home last night.' She paused. 'I think he was worried in case you did something stupid. He's telephoned three times already this morning to see if I've heard from you.'

Kate came to a decision in that moment, and stood up. 'You can call him back and tell him that you have—as soon as I've gone.' She wrote quickly on her notepad, ripping off the top sheet to hand it to the other woman. 'You can reach him on this telephone number,' she said flatly.

Her secretary glanced down, frowning deeply as she looked up again. 'But this is the Melford number.'

Kate walked to the door. 'Did Jared forget to mention that little fact to you too?' she said bitterly. '*He* is Melfords, Jared Rourke Melford.' Her mouth twisted. 'I don't know his extension, but I'm sure the switchboard will put you through.'

'He gave me his home number ...' Beryl said dazedly.

'Well, now you know who you'll be talking to!'

'Yes. But—You—Where are you going?' the other woman seemed to realise Kate was leaving—and that she had no idea where she was going!

'Away for a few days,' Kate answered bleakly. 'I need to be on my own. Please tell Jared I don't want to see him again, I'm sure he'll understand this time.'

Beryl shook her head. 'Not if last night is anything to go by!' she said.

Kate's expression hardened. 'Then I'll just have to stay away until he does.'

Until she knew Jared was pursuing her the idea of running away hadn't occurred to her, but she was too vulnerable at the moment to fight him and any relationship he cared to offer her. She had to get away, as far away as possible, from Jared and the temptation to give in to her love for him.

The hotel was much more crowded in midsummer

than it had been in March, but Kate still managed to keep pretty much to herself, most of the other guests seeming to be family groups intent on enjoying themselves, leaving Kate to her solitude as she made it obvious she required privacy, spending a lot of her time walking alone along the beach as she had before.

Again there were memories of Jared here, but it was for just that reason that she had thought he wouldn't look for her here—and he hadn't. For just over two weeks, two long weeks, she had remained here undisturbed. And she was still no nearer understanding why he had been so deliberately cruel. Perhaps the way she had dismissed him when he sought her out had irked him, made him seek revenge, or maybe, as she had already thought, he found her a challenge he wanted to dominate. Whatever his reason, he had hurt her more than she could bear.

The nights were lighter now, but she was still the only guest who took advantage of late-night walks along the hotel's private beach, often sitting on the golden sand and watching the horizon until the sun disappeared in a spectacular sunset. It was on just such an evening almost three weeks after she had so hurriedly left London that she sensed that for once she didn't have this private beach to herself, that someone else was walking along the sand towards her.

She stood up quickly, brushing the sand from her denims before turning to leave, walking straight into the solid wall of a man's chest.

'Did I startle you?' the man queried softly.

Kate stiffened at the similarity to another conversation that had taken place here four months ago. 'I——'

'I didn't think you could startle pixies,' he drawled mockingly as she looked ready for flight.

A terrible sense of *déjà vu* washed over her. 'Please—leave me alone,' she gasped.

'No.'

'I want to go back to the hotel——'

'Why?'

'I just do.' She wrenched out of his arms. 'Leave me alone. Let me go!'

'No,' he repeated abruptly.

'I shall scream——' God, even she was doing it now—this sounded like the re-run of an old tape!

'Who would hear you?' he taunted.

This was all like the repeat of some horrendous nightmare, and she wasn't at all sure she *wasn't* going to scream after all!

'Your answer is "I didn't come alone",' Jared reminded her softly. '"I came with a friend".'

'But I didn't!' She faced him across the sand, her stance defensive.

'You would have done if you had told me where you were going,' he told her grimly. '*I* would have come with you.'

'I don't think of you as a friend,' she scorned bitterly.

'How do you think of me?' he queried softly.

'As a rich man who likes to play games—hurtful games.' She looked at him coldly. 'Excuse me.' She turned and began walking up the sand towards the hotel.

Jared fell into step beside her. 'I'll walk with you.'

'We've just played this game,' she bit out tautly.

'Then you remember how it ends.'

Kate turned to glare at him, still walking, hurrying her pace a little. 'Anything we had ended just over two weeks ago.'

'Not to me,' he bit out. 'Do you realise the hell you've put me through since you left like that?' he groaned. 'I've looked for you everywhere I could think of. I even flew to Gibraltar to see your parents——'

'You did *what*?' That stopped her in her tracks, breathing deeply as she stood illuminated in the lights streaming from the hotel windows. 'Why on earth did you have to worry them?' she demanded impatiently. 'I'm twenty-four years old, the last thing I would do is run crying to my parents!'

'I knew that after the first five minutes of being with them; they obviously had no idea you'd disappeared from London.'

'They didn't,' she corrected pointedly.

'They still don't,' Jared shook his head. 'I told them I was a friend of yours, that I was over there on business and had promised you I'd look them up.'

'And they believed you?' she scorned.

He shrugged. 'I can be very convincing.'

'So I've noticed,' Kate derided coldly. 'Well, you've seen me now, Mr Melford, so I would appreciate it if you would just leave again.'

'I can't do that, Miss Collins,' he deliberately stressed the false surname she had given him when they were here last time.

She flushed. 'My deception was nowhere near as cruel as yours was.'

'It was worse,' he told her curtly. 'You deliberately lied to me, I just automatically gave a name I'd answered to for almost thirty years——'

'Before you took the name Melford and threw your grandfather out of his own business!'

His mouth twisted. 'My grandfather is alive today for the simple reason that he was ordered by his doctor not to return to work. He's still going strong at seventy-six, he jogs every day, swims, travels—but he doesn't involve himself in the company that almost killed him.'

'Richard said——'

'Richard said a lot of things, by all accounts,' he nodded grimly. 'And not all of them were entirely accurate. But a man who has just been told by you that you don't intend marrying him is allowed a little poetic licence in his jealousy.' He looked at the bareness of her left hand in challenge.

'None of this excuses the fact that you made no effort to correct the mistake about your name, that you let me think you were some out-of-work, out-of-date hippie!'

His mouth was tight. 'I didn't correct the former assumption because I could see you really believed the latter. And you made it pretty clear you wouldn't even think of marrying a man like Jared Rourke,' he reminded her tautly.

Again Kate flushed at the rebuke. 'I don't want to hear any more of this. And if you won't leave the hotel then I'll have to.'

'Why?' he grated.

'Because after the lies you told me, what you put me through, I don't ever want to see you again!'

'I love you.'

His quietly spoken words halted her for only a second, her stride all the more determined as she entered the hotel and went up to her room. Did Jared really think he could make a fool out of her again?

As the lift doors opened on to her floor she stepped forward, only to come to a stop in the corridor. Jared was there before her, leaning against the door-frame to her room—and looking for all the world as if he had been doing it for some time.

Kate stiffened her shoulders, taking the key to her room out of her hip pocket, her hair very red against the dark green tee-shirt she wore, her bared breasts clearly visible beneath the clinging material. 'So you've just proved how fit you are,' she mocked as she unlocked the door.

'Four flights of stairs in ten seconds,' he nodded, not even breathing hard. 'Not bad at all.' He followed her into the hotel room. 'I suppose all these rooms must look the same,' he shrugged. This room was almost identical to the one they had shared four months ago.

'I'm sure you have one of the suites up on the top floor,' Kate said with sarcasm. 'As you did last time.' The last was stated as a question.

Jared nodded. 'I did the last time I was here,' he conceded. 'Although I didn't use it much. I don't happen to be booked in this time.'

'Then it will be easier for you to leave, won't it?'

'I'm not going anywhere without you,' he told her tautly.

'And I'm not going anywhere *with* you,' she snapped. 'We both know exactly who each other is now—and quite frankly I preferred Jared Rourke!'

'I realised that when Richard told me you'd given him back his ring even after he'd taunted you about my never marrying you.'

'Jared *Melford*,' she corrected with some bitterness.

'Jared Rourke and Jared Melford are one and the same man,' he rasped. 'And we both love you and want to marry you.'

She clasped her hands together to stop them shaking. 'I don't believe you. I don't *want* to believe you. You made a fool of me once, Jared, I'm not about to repeat the experience. I don't know why you followed me—What's that?' While he had been talking he had pulled out his wallet and taken out a slip of paper.

'Read it.' He thrust it at her, putting his wallet away again as she slowly unfolded the sheet of paper.

She read it quickly, moistening suddenly dry lips. 'It's a marriage licence,' she croaked.

'What date does it have on it?' he prompted.

She scanned the sheet. It was dated for March, only three days after she had left the hotel so abruptly last time. She looked up at him dazedly. 'You were that confident——'

'I was that sure, of my love for you.' Jared made no effort to touch her, to come closer to her. 'But you were just recovering from an unhappy love affair, I didn't want to be the man you fell for on the rebound.'

'Like Richard . . .'

He nodded. 'At that time I had no idea you'd actually been hurt as much as you had, although the indentation on your ring finger seemed to indicate a serious relationship. But two engagements, obviously to two completely wrong men——'

'That's conceited!' Her anger was beginning to fade, although there was still a lot to be explained before she even dared think of letting her love for him flower once more.

'——made me hope that a third man could be the right one,' he finished as if she hadn't spoken. 'But not Jared Melford, it had to be Jared Rourke. You'd made a decision to marry a man who could give you the power and success Brian had left you and married Coral for. I couldn't be married for those reasons, Kate,' he shook his head. 'I believed that last weekend that you loved me, and yet a doubt lingered. What if my being Jared Melford meant more to you than just loving me? I couldn't accept that,' he said raggedly. 'Hence the pretence right to the end. Then that evening you were going to see Richard to tell him about us you chose me, Jared Rourke, over both him and your career. I tried to tell you the truth then, but——'

'I was in too much of a hurry to listen,' she finished softly, remembering well how he had even followed her out to the lift in his effort to tell her something he thought important. If only she had stopped to listen, none of this would have happened—or would it? Hadn't he still deceived her, lied to her, taken all she had to give and left her with nothing, not even her pride?

'Yes,' he sighed. 'And then you called me from Richard's—or I thought it was Richard's,' he gave her a reproving frown, 'and told me you'd decided on a successful career and a rich husband after all. If you did that I'd been going to use the only card I had left to play,' he said heavily. 'The contract with Melfords.' He met her gaze steadily.

'You were prepared to offer me that contract just to keep me as your mistress?' she gasped.

Jared's mouth tightened. 'Not quite,' he bit out. ' told Harkness to hold off on signing the contract in the event that if you did change your mind and decide to marry Richard I could offer you the contract in exchange for becoming my wife. By that time my pride had gone out of the window! But before I had the chance to do that you told me you were spending the night with Richard. That was too much,' he told her grimly. 'But after I'd stormed through the fla packing my things, some of my frustrated anger had evaporated, and I could see things more clearly. I had to try once more with you, even if it meant you still said no. I telephoned Richard's flat and asked to tal to you. That was when he told me he had no idea where you were, and that he didn't particularly car either. I threw my things in my car——'

'A red Lamborghini,' Kate said dryly.

'Yes.' He looked puzzled by the vehemence of her statement, shrugging it off with a shake of his head. ' went to see your ex-fiancé. And as he gloatingly recalled your conversation—man to man,' he added hardly, 'I knew exactly why you'd gone. After telling Richard—in no uncertain terms—that he wouldn't be guest at the wedding, I left to look for you. I was frantic, searched London for you like a madman. even went to see Linton,' he recalled grimly.

'Brian?' she gasped. 'But I would never go to him

'No,' Jared rasped. 'I knew that as soon as I walked

in on him and Coral having a slanging match. I left when Coral began throwing things at him,' he grimaced.

Kate could feel no sympathy for the unhappy couple; she knew they had made their own hell with their petty jealousies and vindictive natures. She just thanked her guardian angel for saving her from such a marriage with Richard.

Jared sighed. 'No one seemed to know where you were, and for the last two weeks I've had people checking at airports and ports of call for someone of your description leaving the country. It didn't even occur to me to look for you here, not until this morning. A telephone call confirmed that you were indeed here. The Lamborghini has never been driven so fast!'

Kate frowned. 'This hotel doesn't seem like the sort of place Jared Melford would stay at,' she mocked. 'So what were you doing here when we first met— escaping an unhappy love affair of your own?'

'No,' he laughed. 'You remember the conference . . .?'

'That was for Melfords?' she said disbelievingly.

'I'm afraid so,' he admitted with another grimace. 'I got here a few days early, much in need of a rest after a gruelling six months in London. I was glad I had when you arrived, it was love at first sight on my part. And although you didn't love me in return you did like me, felt more than just physical desire, otherwise you would have left after our first night together,' he said confidently. 'But the trip to the States was urgent, I had no choice but to go, and I knew that the mood you were in it was no good trying to tie you down to me before I went; you just weren't interested. You can imagine my surprise when I tried to call you in London the night you left, only to find there was no Kate Collins. I had some people track you down to Kate Collier, told Harkness to put feelers out to your agency for our advertising contract, and after that it was just a matter of waiting until I got back to England before paying you a surprise visit. I had intended showing you the marriage licence that night and marrying you before the end of the week. But the surprise was on me,' he bit out. 'Richard James put his ring on your finger and you made it obvious I wasn't good enough for you!'

'Jared——'

He shook his head. 'Let me finish, Kate. And when I have, if you still want me to go then I will. Colin obeyed instructions about the advertising, and he received a résumé from you. Unfortunately he hadn't taken me seriously, believed I was just bestowing favours on a mistress,' his mouth twisted. 'As soon as I got back I made him realise that wasn't the case.'

'Then that's why he suddenly changed his mind about seeing me! Was it you who telephoned while I was there too?'

'Yes,' he nodded. 'I was upstairs in my office, and I knew Colin resented my interference in a sphere that's been under his control for too many years to number, that he resented you too. But I'm afraid it was the ring on your finger and the news that you were getting married that really shook him.'

'He thought I was marrying you!' Kate gasped in realisation.

'And aren't you?' His blue-eyed gaze held her gold one.

She looked at him wordlessly for several tense seconds. 'You'll never believe I married you because I love you,' she shook her head. 'You'll always believe I married Jared Melford,' she realised sadly. 'Look how you mistrusted me before, so much so that you thought me totally mercenary.'

'Past tense, Kate,' he dismissed. 'If that was what you wanted, to marry Jared Melford, you would have come back to the flat that night and carried on as if nothing had changed. You ran *away* from Jared Melford, will you run back to Jared Rourke?' He held out his arms to her.

With a choked cry she ran into them, burying her face against his chest, feeling his arms tighten painfully about her.

'I love you, my Katharine Mary,' he groaned.

'I love you too—whatever your name is.' She looked up at him tearfully.

His lips claimed hers in a kiss of raging desire that threatened to sweep away all words. But before it did, 'Will you marry me, Kate?' He framed her face with his strong hands, his gaze intent.

'Yes!' she glowed unhesitantly.

'And I do mean marry me, as soon as possible,' he told her firmly. 'There's going to be no engagement; I can't risk your changing your mind.'

'No third time lucky?' she teased, breathless with happiness.

'No,' he said arrogantly. 'I'll buy you an engagement ring after the wedding,' he promised throatily. 'And just to show you how much my grandfather resents my taking over Melfords—he wondered if you would do him the honour of wearing my grandmother's wedding ring.'

Kate's eyes widened. 'He knows about—us?'

Jared's mouth quirked. 'I should think the whole of London knows,' he said self-derisively. 'I haven't exactly been making a secret of it, raging about like a demented bull. Actually it was my grandfather who made me think of trying here,' he revealed with a smile. 'He reminded me of the fact that women are totally illogical——'

'He sounds as arrogant as you!'

'He is,' Jared grinned.

'Then I'm sure I shall love him too,' she smiled.

'And he'll love you—especially when you present him with his first great-grandchild,' Jared teased.

Delicate colour flooded her cheeks. 'Is that—imminent?'

'Very,' he growled. 'After the hell you've put me through I can't hold back much longer.'

Kate lovingly touched his lips with her fingertips. 'You have no need to. We can stay here as long as we want to,' she said dreamily. 'We never have to leave if we don't want to.'

Jared grimaced regretfully. 'I'm afraid we do,' he told her with some reluctance.

'Oh, of course,' she frowned. 'You can't leave Melfords without their Chairman.'

'To hell with Melfords,' he dismissed carelessly. 'My grandfather is arranging our wedding for tomorrow.'

'But——'

'On my instructions,' he put in quickly.

Indignation warred with love—and the latter won easily. 'Arrogant, arrogant man,' she murmured as she raised her mouth to his.

'A man who loves you more than life itself,' he corrected huskily.

'You are my life, Jared,' she told him with quiet sincerity. 'All of it.'

'And that's the way it's going to stay,' he vowed.

Harlequin® Plus

CAESAR SALAD

For her celebration lunch, Kate chooses a favorite spot – a small Italian restaurant "where the food is good and not too expensive, and a table always available." Perhaps, besides enjoying some delicious pasta, Kate and Jared also share a Caesar salad, a perfect accompaniment to pasta. Below is a recipe for Caesar salad for two that you can share with the man you love. (We guarantee it's as good as any you'll get in a restaurant!)

What you need:

Romaine lettuce, washed and torn into pieces
1/4 tsp. salt
3 cloves garlic, peeled
3 tinned anchovy filets, oil rinsed off
1 egg
2 1/4 tsp. lemon juice
1/2 tsp. dry mustard
dash Worcestershire sauce
4 drops Tabasco sauce
3 tbsp. olive oil
freshly ground pepper
1/2 cup freshly grated Parmesan cheese
3/4 cup croutons

What to do:

Sprinkle salt in a large wooden salad bowl. Add garlic and mash to a pulp with the back of a large spoon. Lightly scrape most of pulp from bowl and discard. Add anchovies and mash to a pulp (do not discard). Add egg and beat with fork. Add next six ingredients and combine thoroughly with a fork. Add lettuce, Parmesan and croutons, and toss until lettuce is well coated with dressing.